Paints and Poltergeists

Nola Robertson

ISBN: 978-1-953213-24-2

Also by Nola Robertson

Tarron Hunter Series

Also Available

A Cumberpatch Cove Mystery

St. Claire Witches

Hawkins Harbor Cozy Mysteries

CHAPTER ONE

There were benefits to living in the apartment above Mysterious Baubles, my family's shop. Besides the rent-free agreement I had with my parents for managing the store, getting to work took less than five minutes.

Of course, nothing in life was truly free, and my home came with the stipulation that I kept my grandmother, lovingly known as Grams, out of trouble whenever my now-retired parents traveled. A task that normally would have been easy if the woman didn't possess some eccentric qualities, like sharing psychic predictions and having a penchant for getting herself, along with my friends and me, into trouble.

I'd finished pouring my second cup of coffee for the morning and turned to find Barley, my Kurilian Bobtail, sitting on the back of the couch. He was a gray and black-striped version of a wild cat, minus a tail, and always looked like he was having a bad hair day. Every few seconds, he'd stand on his back legs and paw the frame of the seaside painting hanging on the wall.

"Barley, leave that alone," I said, taking a couple of steps in his direction. He didn't find me intimidating or take my warning seriously. He thought I wanted to play and scampered off the back of the couch and underneath a nearby cushioned chair. It was the third time this morning I'd given him a similar scolding, but this time he'd managed to misalign the frame, so the right side was hanging lower than the left.

We'd been living together for months, and he'd never messed with the painting before. I had no idea why he'd suddenly found the picture painted by the previous tenant so interesting. Though thinking about Roger Nelson's death still saddened me, I smiled every time I remembered how he used to torment Grams. His favorite pastime was coming down to the shop and complaining that he could hear the bell above the front door every time it jingled. In all the years I'd inhabited my apartment, I'd never once heard any noises made by the bell.

I glared at Barley and wiggled my finger. "Any more misbehaving from you, mister, and you won't get kitty snacks for the rest of the day."

He laid on his belly and looked up at me as if he knew I'd never follow through on my threat. He was probably right, but I was determined to show him I meant business. After setting my cup on the kitchen counter, I walked to the couch and knelt on the cushions to straighten the frame.

The instant my fingertips brushed against the dark wood, I felt an electrical shock that pulsed through my hand all the way to my elbow. With a squeal, I pushed off the couch backward. Being athletically inclined wasn't one of my better skills, and I lost my footing when the back of my leg caught on the edge of the coffee table. The way I landed on the floor was less than graceful, made a loud thump, and caused a sharp jolt to radiate across my backside.

Thanks to some recently acquired and unwanted abilities I'd received after being zapped by a spirit seeker, a birthday present from my father, I knew the unexpected shock was a precursor to a visit from a ghost. I might be more receptive to their visits if I didn't always experience some pain beforehand.

I rubbed my tingling wrist and glared at Barley. It was bad enough that my friends and family were happy to unite me with the recently departed, but now it seemed my cat was doing his best to help. "You did that on purpose, didn't you?" I had no proof that my cat actually knew I'd be summoning a spirit by touching the picture frame, but it made me feel a little better to have someone to blame.

Barley acted as if he was oblivious to my accusation. He crawled out from under the chair and rubbed against my leg, his loud purr a show of affection and meant to soothe me.

I was still a novice when dealing with the paranormal, but I did know for certain that the spirits I interacted with didn't die from natural causes. I also knew the only way to open the lines of communication between the undead and me was to touch something they owned or had recently come in contact with.

The picture had hung on the wall for years. I was a decent housekeeper, but the painting only got an occasional dusting, the last one months ago and before my encounter with the seeker. Barley had been the only one to touch, or rather paw it, lately.

Roger Nelson, the artist who'd painted it, had died from a heart attack while eating an ice cream cone during his daily walk through the park. I was sure that qualified as natural causes, so I didn't know whose ghost would appear, and I was a little apprehensive about finding out.

Luckily, I didn't have to wait long. As soon as I pulled myself off the floor and started rubbing the sore spot underneath the black pants covering my backside, the temperature in the room chilled dramatically. Barley had fur, so the frigid air didn't seem to bother him, not that his behavior had changed during any of my previous ghostly visits.

A shimmering light appeared in the middle of the living

room, then gradually transformed into Roger. He wasn't the bright translucent blue I'd come to expect from a spirit, rather a faded version of the tall, lanky man I remembered. He was wearing a cardigan sweater over a button-down shirt that I'd seen numerous times before. Even his hairstyle was the same. The thin, light blue strands, which were silver when he was alive, were combed back to cover his balding head.

"Mr. Nelson, I thought you…"

"Died. I know." He scowled.

"Actually, I was going to say moved on." Before he could respond, an even worse thought occurred to me, causing the muscles in my chest to constrict and making breathing difficult. "Have you been hanging out here all this time?" I asked, afraid that he'd seen me in the shower naked or watched me while I was sleeping.

He must have picked up on the direction of my thoughts and wrinkled his nose. "No, I would never… I've been in the park ever since I died."

I'd forgotten how persnickety he could be. He'd done too many nice things for my family and me when he was alive for me to believe his disgruntled reaction was an act.

"And, just so you know, it wasn't any fun. It's not like new spirits get a welcoming party or anything, and it took some time to figure out what had happened to me. After that, all I could do was watch people going about their business and enjoying their day." His voice held a hint of sadness. The experience must have been horrible and lonely. I couldn't imagine how I'd feel if I had to spend years without being able to talk to anyone or participate in the world around me.

"What I don't understand is how I ended up here and how you can see me," Roger said. "Up until now, I haven't been able to go anywhere else."

Hearing I hadn't been spied on all these years was a relief and the pressure clamping my chest eased.

"Wait a minute," he said, furrowing his thick brows. "I

don't remember you being able to talk to ghosts. At least not that you ever mentioned."

Though I couldn't recall discussing the paranormal with Roger in the past, he seemed perfectly willing to accept its existence.

"It's a fairly new skill," I said, leaving out that it was an ability I hadn't fully mastered yet.

"How does one go about obtaining that kind of skill?" Roger crossed his arms, expectantly waiting for me to answer.

I'd seen the same determined look on my grandmother's face to know I wouldn't get any information out of him until he received an explanation. I spent the next five minutes giving him a brief summary without going into descriptive details about the spirit seeker or what I referred to as the blue tendrils of death that had bestowed me with my new ghost-seeing skills.

Other than telling him I'd encountered other spirits and helped them after their unfortunate deaths, I didn't give him any information about each occurrence.

"If I understand correctly, then you're supposed to assist me so I can move on, right?" Roger asked.

"Basically, yes." I picked up Barley because he'd gone from rubbing the side of my leg to pawing my pants. "I know it's been a few years since you died." Eight, if I remembered correctly. "So, in order to help you, I'll need more details."

He narrowed his gaze. "What kind of details?"

"Pretty much anything you can remember would be helpful." I scratched Barley's head behind his ears. "Like why everyone, including the EMTs, assumed you'd died from a heart attack."

"Because I did have a heart attack," Roger growled. "One minute I was licking a strawberry ripple ice cream cone, and the next I was on the ground feeling like someone had placed a boulder on my chest. I didn't realize I was dead until the medical people arrived, and I was standing off to the side staring at my body sprawled on the ground."

I knew some toxins simulated heart attacks. Was it possible Roger had been poisoned and didn't know it? But if that was the case, wouldn't one of the EMTs have noticed and reported his death as suspicious? "Is there anyone who might have wanted you dead?" I asked. Roger wasn't overly friendly, but I couldn't come up with a reason why someone would want to kill him.

"I think it was someone who wanted my treasure," Roger said.

"Your treasure?" I asked.

Growing up in an area filled with pirate lore, I wasn't surprised that an image of a wooden chest filled with gold coins popped into my mind. It was also something I'd expect to hear from someone who'd lived three hundred years ago, not from an elderly man living in this century.

History books were stuffed with information about the pirates that visited the Maine coast line where Cumberpatch Cove, my home since birth, was located. Many locals speculated that pirates had buried their stolen booty in the area, but as far as I knew, no one had ever found anything near our town.

Banging on the door leading to the stoop and staircase outside startled me and interrupted my thoughts. Jade, one of my best friends, bellowing, "Rylee, are you all right?" made me jump even more and caused Roger to disappear. It also scared Barley, who left scratches on my chest and arms when he squirmed to get away and take refuge underneath the kitchen table.

"I'm fine," I said after unlocking and opening the door.

Jade wore a sliming black dress with a floral print made up of dainty white flowers with yellow and teal centers. She'd accessorized with two-inch heels and pearl-shaped earrings in a matching shade of teal.

"Are you sure?" Jade asked, giving me a once over before stepping inside. "We heard a loud bang downstairs, and Grams is convinced we're having an earthquake. She sent me up here to check on you."

Our town didn't experience earthquakes, so I didn't know why my grandmother always associated them with unusually loud or unexplained noises inside the building.

"Barley was playing with my painting." I waved my hand in the general direction of the living room. "When I straightened the frame, the darned thing zapped me. The banging noise you heard was me tripping over the coffee table and landing on the floor."

Jade raised a brow and cast a blue-eyed gaze around the room. "When you say zapped, do you mean…"

I nodded. She already knew what getting an electrical jolt from an object meant and didn't need an explanation.

"Can I assume it wasn't Barley I heard you talking to right before I knocked?" she asked, then grinned.

Jade, as well as Shawna, my other best friend, never failed to demonstrate their excitement every time I encountered a new spirit. They were always supportive and ready to help me do whatever was necessary to transition a ghost to the afterlife. It was why I didn't have a problem sharing the information with them.

"You can," I said. "My newest visitor is Roger Nelson."

"Why does that name sound familiar?" Jade snapped her fingers and widened her eyes. "Wasn't he the old guy who used to live here before you did?"

"Yeah," I said.

"Is he still here?" Jade asked, glancing around. So far, I was the only one who could see spirits, but it didn't stop my family and friends from checking out the area, hoping to catch a glimpse of my ghostly visitors.

"No, he poofed out when you knocked on the door." New spirits had a tendency to disappear when they got startled. Obviously, Roger had been in our realm for a while. I didn't know if he'd been frightened or had another reason for leaving.

7

"Wait a minute," Jade said. "Didn't Roger die from a heart attack like eight or so years ago? If his death wasn't suspicious, how are you able to see him? And what is he doing here now? Doesn't there have to be a body?"

Jade was usually more perceptive. I was surprised it had taken her so long to make the body connection. Not having a corpse was only one of the many things troubling me about Roger's appearance. "That's what I thought, too," I said. "Until he told me he was murdered."

"How is that even possible?" Jade asked. "Wouldn't it be tough to make a heart attack look like natural causes?"

I shrugged. "I have no idea, at least not yet. Before Roger left, he did say he believed his murder had something to do with his treasure."

"When you say treasure… Do you mean something buried, like a chest?" Jade asked.

"I wish I knew." I leaned against the kitchen counter. "He disappeared before I could get any more information from him."

"So, for all we know, it could be anything." Jade tapped her chin. "It would have to be something valuable, something that someone would be willing to kill for."

"I agree," I said. "And judging by Roger's previous and modest lifestyle, there's no way of knowing what it could be until we talk to him." Which meant I'd have to wait until he showed up again.

I walked over to the counter and picked up my cup, the coffee now too cold to enjoy. I wasn't interested in reheating it, so I emptied it in the sink and rinsed it out. After grabbing Barley's leash, I knelt next to the table and clipped it to his collar. Once I had him nestled against my chest, I said, "We'd better get going before Grams assumes something bad happened and decides to come looking for us."

"You mean worse than an earthquake?" Jade chuckled as she headed for the door.

"Exactly," I said, slipping the strap of my purse over

my shoulder and engaging the door's lock. As I followed my friend down the stairs, I thought about the one thing I knew for certain.

If someone had ended Roger's life, then it was up to me, along with the help of my friends, to find them.

CHAPTER TWO

The bell hanging over the front door tinkling non-stop for more than a minute wasn't an everyday occurrence. Actually, it wasn't something I ever remembered happening. Sitting at my desk in the shop's office and trying to finish paperwork was hard to do when the constant jingling broke my concentration and had reached the level of annoying. Since my parents were checking out a new paranormal museum in Portland, and Jade had left early to run some errands, Grams and I were the only ones working in the shop.

Either we were having an unusual influx of customers—highly unlikely—or my grandmother had to be doing something with the bell. Visions of her being on a ladder had me hurrying to the front of the building.

By the time I reached the end of the corridor, the bell had stopped making noise, and Grams was standing a few feet away from the doorway. She'd gotten a plastic sword from the pirate section and was brandishing it through the air. Grams's short dark hair, liberally sprinkled with silver, was mussed. Swiping at an imaginary foe encompassed her entire body, causing her ankle-length skirt to swish.

"Grams, what's going on?" I asked as I scanned the

surrounding area to make sure there weren't any customers witnessing my grandmother's odd behavior.

"I'm trying to protect the shop." She took another swing and barely missed a shelf lined with souvenir items.

"From what?" I asked. "There's no one here."

"From a magical entity," Grams said. "You need to stay back. I don't want you to get hurt." My grandmother didn't frighten easily, and the worried look she shot at me over her shoulder was enough to convince me she was serious.

"I'm sure there's a reasonable explanation for whatever you think is happening." I thought it was sweet that she wanted to protect me. If there was an actual paranormal event taking place, one I had yet to witness, I wasn't sure why Grams thought she'd be able to ward it off by wielding a child's toy.

Grams turned and pointed the sword at me. "Oh yeah, then explain why objects were moving through the air, and the bell wouldn't stop ringing." She paused to listen, then groaned. "Well, I guess it's not ringing now."

My grandmother might be a bit eccentric and like to embellish the truth, but she was also intelligent and perceptive, so I had no reason to doubt her story. "I heard it too," I said, hoping to reassure her.

Since she was nowhere near the front of the shop and an aisle shelf blocked my view of the door, investigating the malfunctioning bell would have to wait. I was more interested in hearing about the moving objects. "Can you tell me what you saw?"

"I'll show you," she said, straightening her shoulders. Grams aimed the sword in front of her, then took my hand and crept to the next aisle. "There." She pointed at three herbal bottles sitting upright in the middle of the hardwood floor.

I might not have been too concerned if the bottles hadn't been lined up in a row; the spaces between them equally matched. Typically, when Barley knocked the plastic containers off the shelf, they ended up on their sides after he'd rolled around with them.

"Barley didn't do that, in case you were wondering," Grams said.

I knew she was telling the truth because I'd left my cat sleeping on his pet bed in the corner of my office. "Tell me what you saw?" I asked, concerned that she might genuinely have a reason to be upset.

"The bottles floated off the shelf all by themselves." Grams nudged one of the containers with the tip of the sword as if she were afraid it might attack us. "They bobbed up and down in the air, then landed on the floor."

There were three things I knew for sure; I could see ghosts, magic was real, and objects didn't float without help. I immediately thought of Edith and Joyce. The Haverston sisters owned the Classic Broom, and they'd been great about helping me when I first learned I could see spirits. Maybe they could provide some insight into what was happening now.

I was about to grab Grams and head for the phone hanging on the wall behind the cash register when I noticed movement near the front of the store. Movement that transformed into Roger. He stood on his toes, then braced his hand against the wooden frame surrounding the glass on the door, so he could smack the bell with the other.

It hadn't occurred to me that he might be the 'magical entity' Grams had been talking about. None of the other spirits I'd acquired after touching one of their possessions had been able to move inanimate objects. Well, none of them except Martin Cumberpatch, the not so famous pirate our town had been named after. His death resulted from a curse, so most of the rules governing ghosts hadn't applied to him or his situation. Since Roger hadn't moved anything around when he was in my apartment, I hadn't even considered him as a possible culprit.

"Roger," I said. "What are you doing?" What I really

wanted to ask was how he was able to do it. My father had dragged me to plenty of haunted houses, and I'd never witnessed any spirit-supplied activity. I'd seen his abilities firsthand and wondered if magic had played a role in his death. And if it had, how dangerous was helping him going to get?

My question had him pausing mid-swipe, but it didn't stop him from giving me a mischievous grin after muttering "Nothing", then thwacking the bell again. I couldn't believe he'd resorted to such childish behavior. Had being stuck in the park for so long done something to change him?

I didn't have any siblings, but after working summers on my Uncle Max's pirate tour boat, I'd acquired plenty of experience dealing with children. If Roger was going to act like a child, then treating him like one might be the best way to handle the situation.

Using a bribery technique refined by my mother, who I assumed had stolen it from my grandmother, I placed my hands on my hips and said, "If you don't stop smacking that bell, I'm not going to help you."

It wasn't a real threat because not helping Roger meant being haunted by his ghost for the rest of my life, a detail I didn't share. I still had no idea what the treasure was or why Roger thought he'd been killed for it. For all I knew, the treasure was a prized possession like the paints and brushes he'd used to create the artwork hanging in my living room. Maybe even a rock collection. Whatever it was, it held value to Roger.

"I'm sorry," Roger groaned as he lowered his arm.

His apology lacked sincerity, and I had a hard time believing he meant it. When I'd helped Martin, I'd learned right away that establishing rules was necessary. "If we're going to work together, then you can't go around moving objects or scaring people." I wanted to make sure Roger didn't twist my directive to suit his own needs later and added, "And I mean everyone, not just Grams."

"All right," he said, sticking his hands in his front pockets. "I'll behave."

"Rylee," Grams said, drawing my attention away from the ghost. Her confused expression had transformed into a scowl. "Is Roger the one who was moving things and playing with the bell?" She lowered the sword, but only a little. Even though I'd told her about Roger's arrival earlier, it was easy to understand why she hadn't made the connection to him either.

"Yes, and he's sorry for scaring you." I had a feeling, ghost of not, if she'd seen his smirk, Roger would've gotten a few well-placed jabs.

"He should be," Grams huffed, then as an afterthought said, "I didn't know it was possible for regular ghosts to move things."

I didn't have a chance to respond because the bell jingled. I clenched my fists and contemplated how upset my parents would be if I removed it. I turned, ready to scold Roger again, and found Roy Dixon, the town's sheriff, holding the door open as he entered the shop. He was wearing a dark leather jacket over his light tan uniform, which meant he'd probably headed to our place directly from work.

I'd lost track of time and forgotten that Grams and her good friend Mattie, owner of the coffee shop across the street, had plans to go out to dinner with Roy. Something they did on a regular basis. The three of them had been friends for as long as I could remember, but I always suspected that Roy wished his relationship with my grandmother would turn into something more. "Hey, Roy," I said, since I'd known him too long and was way past the point of addressing him as sheriff.

"Good afternoon, ladies," he said, taking a few steps before closing the door.

Roger hadn't moved, so the door, as well as Roy's hand and arm, passed through him. Roy shuddered, then asked, "Is there a problem with your heater?" Even though it was mid-April, we were still experiencing bouts of cold weather. I knew from experience that the temperatures outside didn't cause nearly the chill someone received when coming in contact with a ghost.

Grams and I shared a look, but neither of us commented. He didn't know about my ability, so I couldn't tell him about Roger. And giving him a negative response might elicit an offer from him to check the heating unit, which seemed to be functioning fine.

Roy had the same inquisitive nature as his nephew Logan, who also worked on the local police force as a detective. He'd relocated to Cumberpatch near the end of last summer. He was also my boyfriend and, unlike Roy, was part of a small group of people who knew about my ghost-seeing gift. Logan might be okay with my supernatural ability, but he wasn't thrilled about the investigating that usually accompanied it.

Roy's whiskey-colored gaze intensified the second he noticed the sword Grams was holding, and he asked, "Don't you think it's a little early to be practicing for the pirate festival, or is there something else going on in here?"

"Why would anything be going on?" Grams asked. "I was testing these new swords Rylee ordered to make sure they performed well for the children." My grandmother's feigned innocence never worked on me. And, by the skeptical look on Roy's face, I didn't think it was working on him either.

Roy's arrival didn't seem to make Roger happy, nor did having the door pass through his body. He stepped out of the way and crossed his arms, then glared at Roy as if he'd crashed a private party. "What's he doing here?" Roger snarled. "You didn't tell him about me, did you? Because we don't need his help finding my treasure or my killer."

I didn't know if Roger had a personal reason for not liking the sheriff or if he blamed him for not investigating his death right after it happened. Either way, ignoring

Roger's frowning face seemed like my best option. I couldn't answer his questions, not without Roy thinking I'd conjured up an imaginary being.

I still needed clarification on the treasure issue, as well as the other questions I'd wanted to ask Roger earlier. I decided it might be best to get Roy out of the shop before my unhappy ghost chose to go back on his word and do some misbehaving. "If you guys leave now, you won't have to wait long for a table." I took the sword from Grams. "I don't mind closing up," I added in case she hadn't picked up on my hint.

"That sounds like a great idea," Grams said. "I'll go grab my coat and purse." She gave me a confirming wink, then dashed for the entryway leading to the back of the building.

While we waited for Grams to return, I thought about the circumstances surrounding Roger's death. Until I could do more research, I was going with the premise that if he'd died from a heart attack, I wouldn't be able to see his spirit. If the alternative was murder, then discovering what method had been used might help with uncovering the killer.

Roy had been in law enforcement a long time and might have some useful information. Only asking him about Roger's demise would make him suspicious, so I opted for using a different approach. "Roy, can you answer a quick question before you go?"

Roy leaned against the nearest display counter. "Sure, what do you want to know?"

"Shawna and I were watching a show the other night and got into a discussion about autopsies. She said an autopsy is only done if the death looks suspicious, but I thought an examination was done for every death. Even if, for example, an elderly person appeared to die from a heart attack."

Shawna, Jade, and I did have similar conversations, but we hadn't seen a recent show or discussed that particular topic. I gave him the same sweet smile I'd adopted from Grams, hoping he wouldn't start asking probing questions.

"Shawna's right," Roy said. "If there are no signs of foul play, or someone's death is the result of a medical condition, a disease, or looks like natural causes, then no, an autopsy isn't performed."

"Okay, thanks," I said as my grandmother hurried back into the room.

Grams pulled on her coat, then gave Roy's sleeve a gentle tug. "Are you ready to go?"

"I am," he said, following her to the door.

"If anything important comes up, you know how to reach me. If not, I'll talk to you later," Grams said.

I interpreted the last part of her statement to mean she expected a full report on what I learned from Roger. Knowing my grandmother, she'd probably stop by my apartment on her way home instead of calling or waiting until we got to work in the morning.

"No problem," I said, reaching for the handle and holding the door open. "Have fun, and say hey to Mattie for me."

I watched through the glass and waited until Grams and Roy had crossed the street before turning to Roger. "I'm sorry I couldn't answer your questions in front of Roy. He doesn't know that I can see ghosts. It's not something I share with a lot of people. Right now, my family and a few friends are the only ones who know about my ability."

Actually, the list of people seemed to be getting longer every time I encountered a new spirit. My most recent acquisition was Wesley Macfarland, a deputy from Waxford Bay.

At the rate I was going, it wouldn't be long before everyone in town knew my secret. Though I wasn't quite ready to come out of the proverbial paranormal ghost-seeing closet yet, it was an inevitability my friends continually predicted. It was also the reason they constantly insisted I become a legitimate spirit sleuther. Shawna had even gone online and found a website that provided a certification. Jade showed her support by agreeing with Shawna, at least about getting certified.

I locked the door, then returned the sword to the bin filled with other pirate weapons. I was scheduled to meet with my friends once I finished closing and wanted Roger to go with me, not disappear or cause any more problems. "Do you remember Shawna and Jade?"

He squinted, pondering for a moment before asking, "The cute blonde, and the one who streaks her hair different colors, right?"

I nodded. "Yeah." I wasn't surprised that he'd remembered Shawna and her inclination for adding colorful streaks, which usually coincided with a new season or depended on her mood. The latest shade was a bright blue and also her current boyfriend Nate's favorite color. Getting serious about a guy wasn't Shawna's thing, but the relationship and the hairstyle had lasted a lot longer than the four months Jade and I had predicted.

"They usually assist with my ghostly cases," I said, knowing my choice of words made me sound like the professional sleuther I wasn't. "I'm going back to my apartment to meet with them and see if we can figure out a way to help you." I paused before adding, "I don't suppose you'd like to come with me, would you?"

"Maybe," Roger said. "We'll see." He smirked, then disappeared anyway.

Irritated with the annoying ghost, I groaned, then smiled a few seconds later when Barley padded into the room. He meowed and rubbed against my leg, letting me know it was time to head home.

Cats were fascinating animals. Barley being able to sense the time without using a clock always amazed me. Feeding time was at the top of his list, and if I didn't respond quickly enough, I could count on receiving a reminder that included being pawed with tiny sharp claws.

"Hey, Buddy." I picked him up and cuddled him to my chest as I headed to the back of the shop. As far as I knew, my cat had no idea ghosts existed, yet I couldn't help sharing my troubling question out loud. "Do you get the feeling that dealing with Roger is going to be our most difficult and challenging adventure yet?"

CHAPTER THREE

"Okay, let's have it," Shawna said as soon as I opened the door to let her and Jade into my apartment. "What's the secretive information you couldn't share in your text?" She was carrying three Styrofoam Togo containers and wearing her uniform; a black skirt and cobalt-blue T-shirt with a logo containing a pirate ship and the words "Cumberpatch Cove Cantina" printed on the fabric below her left shoulder. Her blue-streaked, light brown hair was pulled back in a ponytail.

"Jade wouldn't tell me." Shawna shot a sidelong glare at our friend, who'd entered behind her wearing a grin more mischievous than usual.

Since Shawna had been at work when I'd discussed Roger with Jade, I hadn't mentioned him in the message I'd sent telling her I had important news and we all needed to get together at my place when her shift ended.

Shawna had been anxious to hear the latest scoop and offered to supply our evening meal. The restaurant where she worked had some of the best food in town. My friends knew I wasn't much of a cook unless food came prepackaged with instructions, so most of the get-togethers at my place usually involved ordering takeout.

"Well," I said, taking the stack of containers out of Shawna's hands and setting them on the coffee table. For some reason, we always ended up sitting on the sofa and chair in my living room while we ate. More out of habit, and not because I didn't like my dinette table. "I got a surprise visit from Roger Nelson today."

I took a seat on one end of the sofa. Jade opened the plastic bag she was carrying and placed the plastic utensils and napkins on the table, then took a seat in the cushioned chair. Shawna plopped down on the opposite side of the couch and was quickly followed by Barley, who perched between us in hopes of getting a snack. We never fed him scraps, but it didn't stop my cat's efforts.

"Are you talking about the guy who used to live here and always teased me about my hair?" She released an indignant snort. "Um, isn't he dead?" She paused, then glanced, first at Jade, then back at me. "Are you guys saying he came back to life?"

"He's not a zombie," I groaned, then picked up the container with my name scribbled in black marker across the top and placed it on my lap. "He's a ghost."

"How is that possible if he died from natural causes?" Shawna asked, wrinkling her nose. "And what about that thing where you need to touch a dead person's possession to make them appear?" She pinned me with a suspicious glare. "Or, did you find a new way to summon ghosts that you haven't told us about yet?"

"Nope, nothing like that," I said. I'd recently learned that I could also see magical essence on objects and hoped it was the extent of the abilities the spirit seeker had given me. Shawna's excitement about the additional gift included the hope that I'd eventually be able to cast spells or work some kind of magic. So far, I hadn't seen any signs and was happy to disappoint her.

"Roger's painting zapped me." I hitched my thumb at the artwork on the wall behind us.

"How did it manage to do that?" Shawna asked.

"With Barley's help." I frowned at my cat, then scratched his head to let him know I'd noticed him inching closer to my hamburger and fries. "He pawed the frame until it was hanging lopsided. So, when I went to straighten it…"

"You received a magical jolt," Shawna finished for me. After clearing a spot in her container, she opened a ketchup packet and squeezed out the contents. She dipped several fries but stopped before stuffing them in her mouth. "You don't think Roger's been hanging around your apartment and watching you all this time, do you?"

I shuddered. Hearing her say it out loud sounded worse than when the thought had initially popped into my head. "He told me he's been trapped in the park since he died."

"Do you think he was telling the truth?" Jade asked as she spread a napkin across her lap and placed her container on top of it.

"He seemed taken aback when I asked him about it, so yes, I believe him," I said.

"Is Roger here now?" Shawna asked, craning her neck as she gave the room a scrutinizing glance even though we both knew she wouldn't be able to see him if he was there.

"Not yet," I said. "But I did ask him to join us since I'm lacking details and have no idea how we're supposed to help him." I didn't need to ask my friends if they planned to assist me. They were always more than happy to participate.

Shawna treated each of my encounters as a covert mission, which had a tendency to get us into troubling situations. Jade, on the other hand, provided thoughtful insights into any of our precarious predicaments. She also shared the occasional tidbit on appropriate fashion whenever we ended up in the cemetery or other places I deemed scary. Not that I was interested in knowing which shoes were suitable for visiting the undead. No matter how many times Jade insisted my wardrobe needed improvement, which included wearing higher-heeled shoes, I refused to change from being a jeans and T-shirt person on my days off and a casual business person when I was at work.

Shawna finished chewing, then swallowed before asking, "So, if we don't have a body, and Roger didn't move on to the afterlife, are we assuming that he was murdered?"

"That's what Roger thinks," I said. "He was convinced that someone planned his demise because they were after his treasure."

"He had a treasure?" Shawna's confused look was identical to the one Jade had made earlier.

"Yes, I had a treasure," Roger said, his dull blue form appearing in the middle of the room. Only instead of the cardigan sweater he'd been wearing over his shirt the last time I saw him, he had on a black apron with the word "ARTIST" printed in bold across the bib, and a variety of vibrant colors splashed all over the fabric.

If I hadn't been guarding my food from Barley, the container would have flown through the air when he'd startled me. With all the popping in and out my ghostly acquaintances did, my recovery time had gotten a lot better. "Hey, Roger," I said to let my friends know he'd arrived. "I'm glad you decided to join us."

"The place hasn't changed much," Roger said, walking around the room and inspecting as he went. He'd been disoriented and upset during his last visit and hadn't taken the time to notice anything. "What happened to all of my belongings?"

Other than the bedroom set, the rest of the furniture I currently used had been supplied by my parents before they'd rented the space to Roger. I wasn't big on interior decorating, but I'd added a few of my own items to make the place more welcoming. "If you mean your personal things, my mom contacted your sister to come and get them."

Roger's gaze landed on the wall behind me, and he

smiled. "You kept my painting." His choked words sounded more like a question than a statement.

He was a talented artist, and the panoramic view of a beach near the ocean was an exceptional piece of work. I was honored when his sister turned down my offer to buy it and told me to keep it. "I love the colors, and I think it captures the scene beautifully."

Roger had never been good at accepting compliments when he was alive, and it seemed that hadn't changed in death. He hid his appreciation by pursing his lips. I hadn't missed the flicker in his eyes and figured if ghosts could blush, his cheeks would be a bright red. I also remembered him being good at changing the subject and wasn't surprised when he focused his attention on Barley. "What happened to your cat's tail?"

"He's a Kurilian Bobtail, and it's one of his traits." I grinned because my cat had given up on my food and scooted closer to Shawna to focus on hers.

"Is the wild fur specific to the breed as well?" Roger asked.

I giggled. "No, I think the wild look is a Barley thing."

"I see." Roger walked over and picked up one of my cat's toys, of which there were many, off the floor. The majority of them had found a home under my bed, but one or two still made their way into the living room.

Roger tossed the furry catnip-filled mouse across the room. Barley sailed over the coffee table to retrieve it, then captured it with his claws and rolled on his back, giving the toy a cat's version of a bear hug.

Jade and Shawna watched the activity with open mouths.

"Well, that's new," Jade said, referring to Roger's unexpected ability.

Shawna glanced at me. "I know Martin was special because of his curse, but I didn't know regular ghosts could move things around." She stared at the area where Roger was standing, then quickly added, "Not that I'm insinuating you're ordinary or anything."

"I wasn't aware of the skill either, not until we had an incident in the shop," I said.

Roger crossed his arms and smirked. Apparently, he was proud of the chaos he'd caused my grandmother, which proved I was right about his apology.

"Do I want to know what happened?" Jade asked.

"Not really," I said. "Though I will admit that Grams got in some wielding practice with a pirate sword."

"You let her have a real sword?" Shawna asked.

"Like I could ever stop my grandmother from doing whatever she wanted," I said. "No, she snagged a plastic one from the children's section."

"Even so, the thought of Grams running around the shop swiping at anything that moved leaves a mental picture," Shawna said, tapping the side of her head.

Shawna's image of my grandmother trying to protect the shop probably wasn't as good as the real one I continued to visualize in my mind.

"Roger, since you're here, why don't we focus on what we can do to help you," I said, then sealed my container and set it aside so I could grab the pen and notepad off the coffee table. Because of the numerous times my friends and I had brainstormed about my previous spirit encounters, which included coming up with a list of suspects, both items had gotten a lot of use lately. I'd started leaving them out so I wouldn't have to get up and rifle through a drawer.

"It would also help if you told us more about the treasure and why you think someone would want to kill you for it," Jade said. She took a final bite of her sandwich, then crumpled her napkin and tossed it in the container before setting it on top of mine.

"If I tell you about my treasure, how do I know I can trust you not to take it?" Roger asked, tipping his head towards Shawna and Jade. "Or your friends, for that matter?"

"That's not how this works," I said. "My goal is to help you reach the afterlife. If I take your treasure, you won't be able to move on, which means you'll be stuck here forever. Maybe even end up trapped back in the park."

Now that he'd acquired some freedom, he might not be ready to leave, so I neglected to tell him he'd probably be stuck haunting me. After watching him cringe and giving him a few seconds to think about what I'd said, I added, "None of us wants that to happen, which is why we're going to help you."

Jade and Shawna were great about gleaning the gist of my conversations with ghosts. Being more detailed when I talked usually saved me from having to repeat everything I heard. I was glad neither of them said anything and assumed they'd picked up on my fear of a non-stop haunting when I'd mentioned my fabricated speculation about the park.

Roger took a second to consider what I'd said. "Your family has always been good to me, so I'm pretty sure I can trust you to keep your word. Before I tell you how to find my treasure, I want you to promise that you'll hand-deliver it to my niece Erin after you dig it up." He wiggled his finger at Shawna and Jade. "That goes for your friends too."

"When you say dig, do you mean your treasure is buried?" I'd assumed that whatever he'd deemed valuable had been hidden somewhere accessible. In the ground hadn't been a consideration.

"Erin always had a thing for pirates and loved solving puzzles," Roger said. "I'd planned to give her a map for her sixteenth birthday and let her hunt for the treasure."

I relayed what he said to Shawna and Jade.

"So your niece never got to do the search or find the booty." Shawna stuck out her lower lip. "That's so sad."

I didn't think it was nearly as sad as Erin losing her uncle. "Did Erin know about your gift?"

"No, I was going to tell her the same day I died."

Roger mimicked his death by grabbing his chest and rolling his eyes. "But didn't get the chance."

I shook my head for my friends but refrained from sharing his gestures.

"I guess the first thing we need to do is find out if the treasure is still where you left it," I said. Other than my painting, I had no idea what Roger's sister had done with the rest of his stuff. "It would be useful if we had the map, provided it wasn't stolen."

Roger grinned and wrapped his hands around the straps of his apron. "I didn't leave the map lying around where anyone could find it if that's what you're thinking."

"If the map wasn't with your possessions, then where is it?" I asked.

"There is no physical map, not anymore. I shredded my notes after hiding the clues in two of my paintings." Roger grinned. "My niece is smart, and I wanted the hunt to be challenging for her."

After I'd shared the information, Jade asked, "I understand the challenging part, but why two paintings? Why not put all the clues on one?"

"In case someone else tried to figure out the location," Roger said.

"Why would anyone else be interested in clues for a birthday gift?" I asked, still going with the notion that whatever he'd buried would only be special to Erin and him.

"Because the treasure is valuable. Not only personally, but also monetarily." His pale cheeks flushed a darker shade of blue. "I know it was a mistake, but I told some people about the surprise I'd planned for my niece." He glanced at the floor, then mumbled, "They might have gotten the impression that I'd found a map for one of Martin Cumberpatch's buried chests."

That last little tidbit, even if false, would have sparked a lot of interest. Interest worth killing for.

I did another recap, then asked, "If all your precautions

prevented anyone from finding the treasure, then it still has to be where you left it, correct?"

"In theory, yes," Roger said.

"If you show us the location, then we can dig it up and get it to Erin," Jade said.

"I wish it were that easy," Roger said, rubbing his nape. "My memory is a little hazy, and I can't remember exactly where I buried it without seeing the clues first."

I didn't want to embarrass Roger, so I said, "We'll need to find the paintings to locate the treasure."

Jade was the first to glean what I was doing. "Roger, now might be a good time to address any theories you have about your murder."

"It might save us some time if we asked the sheriff to dig up the body and do a special autopsy," Shawna said.

There were times, like now, when my friend's enthusiasm worried me. "No one is digging up anyone's body," I said before Roger could take offense to her suggestion. I thought about the conversation I'd had with Roy. "I doubt Roy will agree to exhume a body without a good reason. It will be hard to prove there was a murder if the authorities ruled the cause of death as natural. We don't have any proof or suspects."

"Oh, we have suspects all right," Roger said.

"We do?" I asked, a glimmer of hope surging through my system. Maybe helping Roger to the afterlife was going to be easier than I'd originally thought.

He nodded. "It had to be someone in my art class. They were the only ones I told about the treasure."

I'd expected one or two names, not an entire group of people. I didn't know if art classes differed in size depending on the course but envisioned the attendees ranging into the twenties.

"Rylee," Shawna said, motioning me to share.

"Sorry," I said. "Roger believes that someone in his art class might be responsible since they all knew about the treasure."

"If one of the other students was the killer, how are we going to prove it?" Jade asked.

"Roger," I said. "Can you remember anything significant that might help us figure out who it was?"

"I think someone went through the supplies I kept in the classroom a few days before I died in the park."

"What makes you think someone went through your stuff?" I asked.

"I liked to keep things organized," Roger said, pacing a few steps. "My paints and brushes weren't in the same order I'd left them after the previous class."

"Was this before or after you shredded the map?" I asked, trying to determine a timeline of the events.

"After, and I'd already added the clues to the paintings," Roger said.

Constantly repeating everything Roger said was exhausting. Nonetheless, I shared the information with my friends. I tapped the pad with my pen while mentally reviewing what I'd learned so far, which wasn't much.

Before we could investigate, we needed to generate a list of suspects and determine what happened to the paintings containing the clues. "Can you tell us how many people were in your class?"

"Names would be useful as well," Jade added.

Before he could answer, my phone started to ring. "Give me a second," I said, then walked over to the kitchen table to retrieve it from my purse. My grandmother's name appeared on the screen. This was no doubt her calling to get an update on my current ghostly situation. "Hey Grams," I said as I turned to face the living room, then groaned when I noticed that Roger had disappeared again.

After letting my friends know we were minus a ghost, I returned to the couch and spent the next five minutes answering Grams's questions. During that time, Barley crawled in my lap and went to sleep. Jade and Shawna cleaned off the coffee table and tossed the containers in the trash.

After disconnecting the call with my grandmother and pushing aside my disappointment about the lack of information, I focused on figuring out how to solve Roger's murder without a body and a list of suspects. "Do you guys think Roger's ability to move things might have something to do with how he died?" I asked.

"Are you thinking magic might have been involved?" Shawna asked. "Because I was."

"Maybe," I said.

"Then it sounds like we need to make a trip to see the spoofers," Jade said, returning to her seat.

There were many things about the situation that I couldn't explain, and seeking expert advice wasn't a bad idea. It wouldn't be the first time we'd sought the help of the spoofers, the nickname we'd given the Supernatural Spoof Squashers, the group that Jade's brother created and organized. Bryce's passion rivaled Shawna's when it came to my ghostly encounters, and he'd been great about providing helpful information on more than one occasion.

"I agree," Shawna said. "If anyone can figure out what happened to Roger, it would be them."

CHAPTER FOUR

My brainstorming session with Shawna and Jade had left me with more unanswered questions. Questions I needed Roger's help to answer, provided the ghost stopped disappearing at inopportune moments. What he'd given us so far was helpful, but it wasn't enough to do any decent sleuthing.

I was curious to know why he could move things when the other ghosts I'd helped couldn't, so Jade's suggestion to seek her brother's help had seemed like the best place to start. With no idea when Roger would reappear, I'd arranged for all of us to meet with Bryce after work the following day.

Since spring had officially arrived, the days were getting longer, and the sunlight hadn't faded from the early evening sky. The drive to Bryce's place had been pleasant. Everyone in our group, which included Grams, was anxious to hear what he'd discovered about Roger's abilities.

With my parents out of town, bringing my grandmother along was simpler than worrying about her causing difficulties elsewhere. Besides, if she hadn't traveled with us, I was certain she'd have shown up anyway and brought Mattie along for backup. When the two women who'd been friends forever got together, there was no telling what would happen. There was a chance Roger would show up while we were at Bryce's place. And since he enjoyed tormenting my grandmother, I figured he might be tempted to stick around so I could finish getting more information.

By the time I'd parked my car in the street in front of Bryce's one-story ranch-style house, he'd emerged from inside and was waiting for us on the porch. At six feet, Bryce stood a few inches taller than his sister. Their facial features might be similar, but Jade's blue eyes and blonde hair contrasted with Bryce's light brown strands and brandy-colored eyes. Like me, he preferred to spend his time outside of work wearing T-shirts and worn jeans.

"Hey, everyone," he said as soon as we started walking along the brick-paved path leading to his porch. "Come on in." He opened the front door and waved for us to enter.

"I really appreciate you doing this for me," I said as I followed after Grams.

"I'm always glad to help," he said.

Being a novice when it came to my paranormal abilities was frustrating. It was great that I could rely on Bryce when I needed answers, but it would be nice if I had a better knowledge base and resources, so I wouldn't constantly have to ask others for help. Maybe Shawna and Jade were right. Perhaps it was time to invest in some additional training.

The foyer led into a living room decorated with a basic set of furniture, light tan walls, and a dark carpet. Most of Bryce's time outside his assistant's job at the local college was spent reading books or in front of a computer, so it always amazed me how tidy he kept the place.

Once we were all inside, Grams asked, "Are your headquarters still in the basement?"

I'd forgotten this wasn't the first time my grandmother had been to Bryce's place. She'd tagged along when we were trying to help Martin.

"Yep, right through there." Bryce grinned and motioned Grams toward the open door on the opposite side of the kitchen.

Bryce went down first, with Grams and Jade following behind him. The last time we'd visited, Shawna had been afraid to descend the dimly lit stairs for fear of finding a dead body when we reached the bottom. A trepidation I hadn't admitted at the time but had also shared. It was one of the few occasions I'd been reminded that my friend had a strong grip. Today, she had no reservations and happily reached for the railing ahead of me.

When I reached the bottom, I glanced around, noting that everything appeared to be the same. The washer and dryer were sitting off to the side in a corner. The rest of the room had been modified into an office and mini living room, complete with a sofa large enough to accommodate three people and a couple of matching chairs.

In the middle of one wall was an old laminated desk; the cushions on the chair sitting next to it were worn and faded. Bryce's state-of-the-art computer system always seemed out of place compared to the rest of the items in the room.

"Where's Nate and Myra," I asked, surprised that the other two members of the spoofers weren't already waiting in the basement for us.

"Oh, Nate's still at work," Shawna said, her voice lacking its usual enthusiasm when she talked about her boyfriend.

Nate was a nice guy, and lately it seemed like things between him and Shawna had reached a serious level. I shared a concerned glance with Jade, who hadn't missed the change in our friend's demeanor either. If they were having problems, it wouldn't take long before Shawna shared the details with us.

"Myra had a family thing she couldn't get out of," Bryce said. "They were both disappointed that they couldn't be here, but I promised I'd fill them in later."

Normally, I wouldn't mind that Myra hadn't been able to make it. She was a bit standoffish and scoffed when she'd first learned about my ghost-seeing ability. We weren't good friends or anything, but after she'd helped with Barley in the pet contest during the vacation Jade, Shawna, and I had taken to Waxford Bay, dealing with her had gotten better.

"After you called about Roger, I did a little research," Bryce said. "I vaguely remember meeting him once, but I have seen some of his work. He is, I mean was, a talented artist."

I thought so too and didn't understand why he was taking the art class he'd mentioned. Maybe it was an advanced class, and he wanted to learn some new techniques. It was something else I wanted to ask when his ghost decided to show up again.

Bryce gazed around the room. "He isn't here now, is he?"

His discomfort about discussing someone when they were in the room and couldn't be seen by anyone but me was understandable. "No, I haven't talked to him since last night," I said. "I'll let you know if he shows up."

"Good, thanks," Bryce said, then asked, "Do you mind answering a few more questions?"

"I don't know much, but if it will help, then sure," I said.

"Other than Martin, is this the first time a ghost has appeared without you seeing a body first?"

I nodded. "Yes."

"And no curses that you know of, right?"

"Correct," I said. As far as I knew, witches were the only ones capable of cursing anyone, and I didn't think Roger had associated with any when he was alive. Though I was pretty sure my friends and I weren't going to be dealing with someone who cast spells, I wanted to confirm my assumption with Roger before checking it off the list.

Bryce walked over to a wall lined with shelves. "And the only time you've seen a ghost was after you got zapped by touching a personal belonging, right?" He furrowed his brows as he studied the rows of books.

"Yes, so far." I leaned with my backside pressed against the edge of his desk.

"Did you see anything out of the ordinary that might indicate Roger had been in your apartment before now?" Bryce said, glancing in my direction before concentrating on his library again.

"Thankfully, no," I said. "If Barley hadn't knocked the picture hanging above my couch sideways, I wouldn't have messed with it and would never have known Roger was stuck in our realm."

"Bryce, do you think there may be other ghosts living in Rylee's apartment?" Shawna asked. The intrigue in her voice outweighed what should have been a concern for my privacy. The thought of being spied on in my home by numerous ghosts was disconcerting, and I joined her in staring at Bryce expectantly.

"I wouldn't think so," he said. "So far, we're assuming your ability to seek spirits is linked to the recently deceased. Well, except for Roger, who appears to be a rare case. You don't have anything else stashed at your place that belonged to a murder victim, do you? Maybe something you haven't bothered to touch yet?"

I glared at Bryce. Did he honestly think I collected random objects to see if they had spirits attached to them? When I noticed the lack of emotion on his face, I realized he'd gone into data collecting mode. None of his questions were meant to be personal. "No, just the painting," I said. "Some of the furniture belonged to my parents, but everything else is mine."

"Then that leaves figuring out what really happened to Roger." Bryce pulled a thick book with a worn leather binding off one of the upper shelves. He walked over to his reading table and gently set it down, caressing the outside before lifting the cover.

"And why he can move things when the other ghosts who visited Rylee couldn't," Grams said. She scrunched her face, no doubt still irritated with Roger for scaring her with his pranks.

I'd already told Bryce about Roger's ability, but he glanced up from reading to acknowledge my grandmother's request with a smile.

"Do you think Roger's circumstances had anything to do with a curse like Martin's did?" I asked.

"I can't say for certain," Bryce said. "Was Roger the type of person who'd go out of his way to interact with or upset a witch?"

"Maybe he's wrong about being murdered. Maybe he stayed around out of sheer determination." Grams snickered. "He could be irritating, but he never mentioned having anything to do with the magical community."

"I hope you're right," Jade said. "Because none of us are equipped to deal with anything that might involve a witch."

"Is there something in your books that would explain how someone could make Roger's death look like natural causes?" I asked. "Something designed to fool the authorities?"

"Hmmm," Bryce said. He slowly flipped through the book, pausing several times to peruse the writing. After a few minutes, he smiled and tapped one of the pages. "I think I might have found something."

"Really?" I asked, moving to stand on his left with Grams while Shawna and Jade crowded together on his right.

"I think he might be a poltergeist." Excitement oozed from Bryce's voice as he pointed to a section on the page.

"A what?" I asked.

"A poltergeist...you know, a spirit who likes to play pranks," Bryce said. "There's not a lot of information here, but it does say they like to move things around, mostly small items, occasionally furniture, and are responsible for loud noises, like slamming doors."

"The prank part definitely describes Roger, all right," Grams said.

Shawna rolled her eyes. "I can't believe I didn't think of it before."

"Think of what?" I asked.

"That Roger must have been the ghost rumored to be haunting the park," Shawna said. "There have been documented sightings of swings moving by themselves, and sandcastles magically appearing overnight in the sandboxes."

"Roger did say he'd been trapped in the park all this time, so you could be right," I said.

"Troy Duncan did an article about it in the Swashbuckler Gazette," Shawna said. "He even posted a picture of the sandcastles."

I remembered reading about the elaborate creations and how local law enforcement, namely Roy, had speculated that the real culprits were local teenagers who'd gotten together in the middle of the night and done it as a hoax.

"I'll bet it was hard being in one place all those years with no one to talk to," Shawna said.

"Does the book mention what types of deaths are responsible for turning someone into a poltergeist?" I asked.

Bryce gently ran his finger along several paragraphs on the book's page. "I'm afraid not, but it does say that poltergeists are rare."

I should have known finding the answer wasn't going to be simple. On the upside, if the appearance of poltergeists wasn't common, then I didn't have to worry about dealing with a lot of them in the future. Or so I hoped.

"If you want, I can reach out to some of my other sources and see if they have more information," Bryce said as he returned the book to the shelf.

There might only be three members in his group, but I didn't doubt Bryce had connections to more paranormal enthusiasts. "I appreciate the help, but I don't want you to go to any extra effort."

"It's no problem," he said. "Now that I've started researching, I'd really like to know more about them myself." He flashed me a wide-toothed grin. "Besides, finding answers about the supernatural is what the spoofers are all about."

I'd never heard Bryce refer to his group by the nickname we'd given them before and giggled. "Then, by all means, research away."

CHAPTER FIVE

I had no idea how long it would take Bryce to find some helpful information or if he'd be able to find anything useful at all. It was seven in the evening when our group left his place and returned to the shop. The more I learned about Roger's situation, the more unsettled I became. I was too anxious to relax, so after Grams headed home, I invited Shawna and Jade to stay and help me do some brainstorming.

I'd barely settled on one end of the sofa with my notepad and pen when a chill rippled through the room. Roger appeared in the middle of my coffee table, his legs below the knees cut off by the wooden surface. He'd traded in his apron for a white smock speckled with a rainbow of different colors. After glancing down, Roger frowned, then took a few steps backward, so he was standing in the room and not in a piece of furniture. "I haven't had too many problems going places," he said in answer to my inquiring look. "It's where I end up once I get there that's still giving me trouble."

"I'm glad you decided to come back," I said to alert Jade and Shawna, which probably wasn't necessary, judging by the way my friends were rubbing their arms and scrutinizing the room.

It usually took the other ghosts I'd helped a day or so after their deaths before they could travel wherever they wanted. It was nice to know Roger fit at least one of the parameters I was familiar with. "I'm also glad you're not trapped in the park anymore," I said.

"Thank you for that," he said and smiled.

Freeing Roger had been an accident, one I wasn't willing to take credit for. "You're welcome, but Barley's the one who deserves your gratitude. If he hadn't been playing with the picture frame and tilted it sideways, I wouldn't have touched it, and you wouldn't be here."

"Then please, thank your cat for me," Roger said, smiling at Barley, who'd curled up on the couch next to me and fallen asleep.

Besides the questions I had about his murder and finding the treasure, I was curious to know more about his ghostly travels. "Do you mind telling me where you went when you left the last time?" I didn't want him to vanish again, so I did my best to sound inquisitive and not like I was berating him for his untimely disappearance.

"Now that I can go places, I wanted to check on my sister and her family," Roger said. "Only when I got to their place, I found other people living there instead."

He paced a few steps, then turned when he reached the kitchen area. "I might have scared the current residents when I opened some doors to check all the rooms in the house."

He tucked his hands in his pockets, trying to appear innocent, an act I wasn't buying. Even if I hadn't noticed the mischievous glint in his eyes, I knew he could've walked through the walls and gone unnoticed. I also wondered if opening doors was all he'd done but decided not to ask.

I shared what Roger had said with the group, omitting his prank or my thoughts on the matter. I didn't think telling Roger about our trip to see Bryce or that he was a poltergeist would be helpful to the situation, so I refrained from mentioning it. At least for the present.

"It's going to be a little hard to give Erin the treasure after we find it if we don't know where she's living now," Jade said. She shifted her weight to lean on the chair's armrest and talk to Shawna at the same time. "Since you enjoy searching the Internet, maybe you can try to find her that way."

The compliment had Shawna proudly sticking out her chest. "I'd be happy to." Then she asked Roger, "What's Erin's last name?"

"Managan," Roger replied happily.

After writing his niece's name down on my notepad, I tore the top sheet off and handed it to Shawna. "Thanks," she said, tucking the paper in her pants pocket. "I'll do some research and let you know what I find."

With that out of the way, it was time to ask my other questions. "Roger, can you remember when you acquired your abilities to move things around?" I couldn't shake the feeling that magic had somehow played an important role in Roger's death. Each new tidbit of information I gleaned seemed to lean in that direction.

"I developed the skill not long after I died," Roger said. "At first, it was little things, like moving a swing a few inches. Over time, I was able to build castles in the children's sandbox."

"You'll be happy to know that the Gazette published an article with pictures showing your sand creations, along with speculations that the park was being haunted," I said.

"They did?" Roger asked.

"I thought your handiwork was spectacular." Shawna smirked, reminding Jade and me that she'd been right about the source of the castles.

To solve Roger's murder, we needed more than speculation. We needed suspects. "Do you know how many people were in your art class?" I asked.

"We could use their names too," Jade added.

41

"Or at least the name of the instructor, if you can remember it," I said as I picked up the pen and adjusted the pad for writing.

"I might be old, dead, and unable to remember where I buried my treasure." Roger scrunched his face as he spoke. "But I can still recall the important things."

"He's thinking" was the translation I gave my friends.

Shawna and Jade shared an amused look, no doubt having similar thoughts to mine.

After a few seconds of patiently waiting in silence, Roger finally answered. "Besides Amos Newsam, the instructor, there was Edwina Gottler, Ethan Atwell, and Polly Hederman."

I didn't know Amos or Ethan, but I did know Edwina and Polly. I had a friendly relationship with Edwina from the many visits I made with Jade and Shawna to Fanciful Threads, her women's clothing boutique. The store was one of Jade's favorite places to shop for clothes.

I didn't have the fashion expertise that Jade did, nor did I enjoy shopping for hours. I went along more to spend time with my friends than anything else, which usually equated to an occasional purchase.

I'd developed an acquaintance with Polly from the numerous times I'd eaten at the Tasty Trinkets, the quaint cafe she owned that was located near the park. The place served sandwiches and had a nice selection of desserts. I hadn't been there in a couple of months, but I'd bet if I checked the menu, I'd find strawberry ripple ice cream listed as one of their flavors.

"I thought there'd be a lot more students," Jade said after sharing the information. I had too and was relieved the suspect list had been drastically minimized.

"It was a class on finger painting with oils, and Cumberpatch only had a few artists interested in mastering the techniques Amos was teaching," Roger said.

I'd always thought paintings were done with a brush and had no idea beautiful artwork could also be created using a person's fingers. Gifted with a curious nature and the need to continually add to my personal knowledge base, I planned to research it later.

I returned my attention to the current topic, and after writing the word "Suspects" at the top of my pad, I jotted down the names Roger had given me.

It was good to finally have a list of people who might have wanted his treasure, but questioning them about it after all these years presented a different kind of problem. Because the locals and visiting tourists embraced the paranormal, possessing eccentricities or magical powers were accepted qualities. My family's shop was well-known and had a good reputation, and I didn't want to ruin it by appearing too nosy about something a killer would want to remain in the past.

So far, I only had Roger's word that one of these people might be responsible for his death. I'd need more information, better yet, some proof, before doing an intense investigation. Finding the treasure and making sure it actually existed would help tremendously.

"We also need to know which two paintings contain the clues," I said. "Can you tell me what they look like?"

"That's easy." Roger pointed at the one hanging on my wall. "You already have one of them, and the second one has a similar setting." He chuckled. "I guess you could say they're a matching set."

"Don't you think you could've mentioned that my painting contained some of the missing clues before now?" I said, scowling at the infuriating ghost. Knowing the information sooner would've alleviated some of the stress I'd been experiencing since he'd popped into my life.

He shrugged, irritating me even more. Shawna and Jade would most likely find Roger's humor entertaining, but I wasn't in the mood to give him the satisfaction by sharing. "Roger said the other painting looks a lot like mine."

"That helps. Now we need to figure out what happened to the other one," Jade said, her gaze locked on the space where Roger was standing. "Any ideas or suggestions about where we should start looking?"

"Yeah," Shawna said. "I'd also like to know how Erin was supposed to decipher the clues if one of the paintings was here and the other was somewhere else."

"My plan was to bring them both here," Roger said. "The framing on the second one took longer than expected. I was going to go by the shop and pick it up after my daily walk in the park." He released a dejected sigh. "But we all know that didn't happen."

"If you didn't pick up the painting, then where did it end up?" I asked, knowing the possibility of the artwork still being at the framing shop was low.

"I had an ongoing arrangement with the store's owner," Roger said. "If I didn't go by to get the artwork myself, they were supposed to deliver it to my workroom at the school."

"If the painting ended up back at the school, then there's a chance Amos or someone else working there knows what happened to it," I said.

"I'd like to make a trip to the school, but before we do, I think we should start talking to the people we know first," I said.

"You mean like Edwina and Polly?" Shawna asked.

"Yes," I said. "I'll take a trip over to see Edwina tomorrow while I'm out running errands, then let you guys know what I find out." I didn't have to explain my reason for wanting to go alone. Jade and Shawna already knew it was easier to get information from a potential suspect if they only had to deal with one person. Sometimes a group, even if it was only the three of us, could be intimidating.

Besides, Shawna was scheduled to work at the restaurant, and having Jade at the shop with Grams gave me one less thing to worry about. Not that my friend could stop my grandmother if she decided to leave the store. The past few days had shown an increase in the tourist business. With any luck, the shop would see another busy day and keep Grams occupied.

Shawna was already getting to her feet to inspect Roger's artwork. I leaned over Barley and touched her arm. "Before we start examining the painting, maybe we should piece together Roger's timeline."

"You mean like the ones the cops use for solving their cases?" Shawna asked as she dropped back into her seat.

"Exactly," I said, turning to Roger. "Can you tell us what you did prior to the incident?" Since he was touchy about discussing his memory, I was careful not to use the word "remember" in my request.

Roger walked over to the kitchen table and pulled out a chair. After he was seated, he asked, "What do you want to know?"

"Let's start with everything you did within the twenty-four hours before you went to the park," I said. Roger had already admitted having a sporadic memory. Maybe walking him through the events of his day would help him recall an important detail we could use. Something that might assist us with finding a quicker resolution.

"Don't leave anything out," Shawna said. "Anything unusual or out of your normal routine, no matter how small, could be relevant."

CHAPTER SIX

After an evening spent obtaining as much information from Roger as possible, I felt better about setting out to do some investigating. Other than spending time in his workshop putting some finishing touches on a painting, there wasn't anything Roger did before his death that sounded unusual.

At some point, I would need to tell Logan about Roger and the possibility that he was murdered. Since there wasn't a body and my research didn't interfere with one of his cases, I hadn't technically crossed any of our relationship boundary lines or done anything to earn one of Logan's don't-get-involved lectures. Until I found something substantial, I decided to put the conversation off as long as possible.

In the meantime, I was going to work through my list of suspects and see if my friends and I could locate Roger's missing painting. An uneasy feeling settled inside me when I thought about Edwina and Polly being involved. Reassuring my friends and myself that they had nothing to do with his death was the main reason I wanted to start with them first.

I'd given Roger until mid-morning to make an

appearance. When he didn't, I headed to Fanciful Threads without him. The store was located several streets south of Swashbuckler Blvd., the town's main street, and shared a block with two other stores. It was too far to walk from my family's shop, so I'd had to drive. The place might not sell any paranormal items or souvenirs to attract the constant flow of tourists that visited Cumberpatch, but the store was always busy every time I visited.

Today was no different. Besides Edwina, there were two other employees helping customers. Both of the women appeared to be in their mid to late twenties and were fashionably dressed. One, a brunette with a short layered haircut, was showing a woman to the dressing rooms near the back of the store. The other had straight jet-black strands and was standing behind the counter ringing up a purchase.

Edwina's outfit matched the stylish clothes found throughout her shop. Today she had on a medium gray ruffle-back blazer that slimmed at her waist and a pair of black pants. The soft curls of her long blonde hair draped naturally over her shoulders and touched the middle of her back.

As soon as she heard the bell above the door tinkle, she hung the dress she was holding on the nearest rack and looked in my direction. "Good morning, Rylee. How are you doing today?"

"Fine," I said, heading in her direction.

Edwina glanced at the glass door closing behind me. "Where's Jade and Shawna?"

"I'm afraid they had to work," I said.

The "Oh" sound she made wasn't surprising, since I rarely visited her place without my friends. "I was out running errands and promised Jade I would stop by to see if you had any sales," I said before she could ask me why I was shopping alone.

I'd discovered that fabricating the truth, even if only a little, came hand in hand with investigating. It was an aspect I didn't enjoy and was glad that what I'd told Edwina leaned toward the side of honesty. Jade had been disappointed that I was making the trip without her, and she'd made me promise to let her know if Edwina was running any sales.

Grams refused to be omitted from my quest to help Roger and had questioned me thoroughly about any progress my friends and I had made the night before. I thought obtaining sales information was a reasonable price to pay for asking my friend to keep an eye on my grandmother. Actually, I knew I was getting the better side of the deal.

"Well, then let me show you what I have." Edwina smiled and motioned me to come closer.

As I followed her to the opposite side of the room, I struggled to find a way to lead the conversation into discussing Roger and the missing painting. She stopped by a nearby rack marked with a large sign designating that all items included a ten percent discount. "Please tell Jade this sale lasts through the weekend."

"I will," I said, giving the rest of the shop a glance. "It looks like you're staying busy."

"Always." Edwina grinned, her gaze taking in the handful of customers perusing her wide assortment of items. Besides the racks filled with women's clothing and undergarments, she also had several display cases filled with accessories and jewelry. "Things have seemed to pick up now that the weather is starting to get nicer."

Discussing any upcoming events in town was the standard conversation starter for those of us who'd been born and raised in the area. Since there weren't any activities scheduled for at least a month, most of the locals reverted to talking about the mundane, which started with the weather, then progressed into the latest gossip.

A few months back, I'd ended up as a hot topic on the rumor circuit because Lavender Abbott, manager of the Beaumont Inn and my nemesis since high school, had witnessed several of Martin's antics and assumed I was the cause.

Listening to rumors was unavoidable. Hearing those that pertained to me, disconcerting. If at all possible, I wanted to keep myself out of the conversation with Edwina in case she'd heard I was a witch when clearly I wasn't.

I surveyed the room once again, hoping to find something I could use to smoothly transition into talking about Roger. Edwina occasionally replaced the paintings on the nearby wall with new ones and had recently changed out two winter scenes with some garden florals. The only painting I remembered from previous visits was a lovely rendition of the Cumberpatch harbor, which appeared to hold an honorary place year-round.

"Are these new?" I asked, moving closer to the paintings.

"I've had them for a while, but it's the first time I've brought them to the shop," Edwina said as she walked over to stand next to me. "I like to display pictures that coincide with the change in seasons."

"Did you paint these yourself?" I pointed at the initials "EG" scrawled in black cursive on the bottom right-hand corner of the floral prints.

"I did," she stated proudly.

"I have to say you're quite talented," I said. "These are both very nice." It was amazing how well the vibrant array of colors Edwina had used complemented the pale mauve walls in her store. "I really like the one with the violet blossoms." I'd never seen that particular flower before and wondered if it was native to Maine. "What kind of plant is it?"

"Thanks," Edwina said. "Its real name is monkshood, but you might have heard it referred to as wolfsbane. I painted this one several years ago. The plants only bloom during the summer."

Wolfsbane sounded familiar, but I couldn't remember

why? Though I suspected the plant might have something to do with the supernatural world? And, if so, did that mean Edwina was somehow linked to the paranormal? I didn't think asking her if she was a witch would be appropriate, so I continued to stare at the painting.

"I don't think these are nearly as good as the one Roger Nelson painted for me." Edwina's voice held a hint of sadness when she pointed at the picture of the harbor.

"I didn't know you knew Roger too," I said, impressed that my lie sounded believable. A few days ago, and before my recent conversation with his ghost, the statement would have been accurate.

"I met him before he passed away," Edwina said. "As a matter of fact, we were taking an art class together."

"Really," I said, encouraging her to share more information.

Edwina grinned. "For a short time, I'd even considered becoming a full-time artist."

"Why didn't you?"

"As much as I enjoy painting, my real dream was to have my own place, so when this boutique became available, I couldn't pass on the opportunity."

"Based on your shop's success, I'd say you made the right choice," I said, trying to remember when she'd gotten the place. I really liked Edwina and hoped that if the treasure was missing, it didn't coincide with the opening of her shop.

"Me too," she giggled, then asked. "So, how did you know Roger?"

"He used to live in the apartment above my family's shop."

"You must have visited with him regularly then," Edwina said.

I smiled, not willing to dispute her assumption or give her a reason to change the subject.

"Did he tell you about his treasure map?"

"He did," I said. "But I thought he was teasing."

She flicked her wrist. "I did as well, especially after hearing a bunch of the locals claim they'd found an authentic map for Martin Cumberpatch's hidden treasure."

Edwina had stated her belief with such sincerity that I found it difficult to believe she'd had anything to do with Roger's murder. Even so, there was still a chance she might know what happened to his other paintings. "I understand that Roger used to have a workshop at the school," I said. "Do you know what they did with the rest of his artwork?"

"I don't, but I'm sure the owner, Amos Newsam, would know," Edwina said.

"Excuse me," a middle-aged woman clutching a dress attached to a plastic hanger against her chest said. "Can you help me, please?"

"Sure," Edwina said, giving me an apologetic look, which I returned with an understanding one of my own.

"I'll talk to you later," I said, reviewing everything I'd learned as I headed for the door.

CHAPTER SEVEN

After my visit with Edwina, I'd returned to the shop, reasonably sure she wasn't aware of any pertinent details regarding Roger's treasure. Determined to move forward with investigating the other suspects on my list, I decided to act on Edwina's suggestion to contact Amos. Once I'd located the number for the Cumberpatch Cove School of Arts, I'd gotten lucky and caught him outside of his class.

It was already Friday, and since there were no weekend classes scheduled, he agreed to an early morning meeting at his coastal home.

Grams had a tarot reading scheduled before the shop opened; otherwise, she would have accompanied me on my trip. Other than mumbling that Amos's wife Sophie could be a little scary, my grandmother wouldn't expound on the reason she'd insisted that I take Jade and Shawna with me. Roger had appeared during my conversation with Grams and had vehemently agreed with her.

I appreciated their concern, but they could've spared me their insistence. I'd already decided to ask my friends to go with me. Questioning potential suspects in a public place with other people around was preferable. Even if I had known Amos, I wouldn't have gone to his home without some kind of backup.

After witnessing Roger's protective behavior, I wasn't surprised when he showed up the next day at my apartment shortly before my friends arrived and informed me he was going with us to Amos's place. Had volunteering to go along been because he wanted to see his old friend or because he was truly worried about my safety?

Usually, I enjoyed the relaxing drive along the two-lane road that wound its way along the coast. Today, however, the prospect of meeting someone for the first time who might be a potential killer had my stomach fluttering in an unpleasant way, not the excited reaction I had whenever I saw Logan. Worrying about Roger and his unpredictable propensity for moving things and frightening people wasn't helping either.

"Roger," I said, glancing in the rearview mirror, glimpsing Shawna first, then smiling at my ghostly passenger. He was taking the investigation of his murder seriously and had gone from wearing artist accessories to disguising himself as a detective, including a trench coat and a plaid deerstalker cap.

"Yes." He stopped staring out the window to give me his full attention.

"I need you to promise that there won't be any shenanigans during our visit with Amos."

He crossed his arms and squirmed in his seat. "I can't promise anything if it turns out he's the killer."

From the information I'd gathered, it sounded like Roger and Amos had been friends a long time. If anyone would know what Amos was capable of, I believed it would be Roger. "Do you think he's the one who did you in?" I asked.

"Not really, but nowadays, you never know." He sighed, then widened his eyes. "What if things go wrong, and you need to be rescued? Would it be all right then?"

I didn't know if Roger coming to our aid would make

matters worse. "I'm sure we'll be fine," I said, then added for Jade and Shawna. "Roger doesn't think it was Amos."

Jade, who was sitting in the front passenger seat, shifted sideways to peer behind us. "That's good to know, but if you were to speculate, who do you think did it?"

It was a good question, one I hadn't even thought to ask.

Roger pursed his lips. "To tell you the truth, I don't know who needed money bad enough back then to want my treasure. Let alone be desperate enough to end my life to get it."

"Since you have no idea, I guess we'll need to continue working through our list of suspects," I said.

"Speaking of suspects," Shawna said, glancing at the direction app on her cell phone. She leaned closer to the window, her face an inch from the glass. "Amos's home should be the next turn on the right."

"Got it," I said, then slowed to make the turn onto a graveled drive.

Amos lived in a beige two-story New England style house. The shutters mounted next to the windows on the lower level were painted a dark brown. The remainder of the exterior trim was done in white. The lawn in the front yard showed signs of green and had a walkway comprised of sandstone pavers cutting through it from the porch to the edge of the driveway.

After parking, I waited for my friends and Roger, who'd exited the vehicle by passing through the car door, to reach the porch before knocking.

Unless we had the wrong address, the woman who yanked the door open and glared at us had to be Sophie. "Who are you?" she asked in a disgruntled tone after taking the time to study us from top to bottom.

Hints of silver layered the dark strands cut short along her forehead, as well as the longer lengths framing her face. Her dark eyes leaned toward beady and were outlined with black mascara. If she hadn't been wearing a nice casual outfit made up of a white long-sleeved blouse and gray slacks to soften the look, I would've believed my grandmother's assessment that Sophie was indeed scary.

"I'm Rylee Spencer," I said, waving my hand toward my friends who were standing on my left. "And this is Shawna and Jade."

"Spencer?" Sophie asked. "Are you related to Abigail?"

"Yes," I said, cringing against the uneasiness skittering through my body. "You know my grandmother?"

"We've met." Sophie sneered.

I'd ascertained as much from Grams. Though I was curious to know what happened during their interaction to cause the negative response, I didn't think I'd get any details no matter how much I pestered either woman.

"You're not from the school." Sophie's glare encompassed all three of us. "So, why are you here?"

"We have an appointment with Amos," I said, straightening my shoulders and doing my best not to let her intimidate me.

Sophie tightened the hand she had braced against the door frame. "Why do you need to see my *husband*?"

Had Amos neglected to tell her about our meeting? Was that why she seemed so agitated? The emphasis she'd made on her connection to Amos was laced with possessiveness. My friends and I hadn't even met the man, so there was no reason for her to be jealous of us.

Did her negative attitude stem from problems in their marriage? Had her husband been unfaithful? Was that the cause of the underlying bitterness? If I'd thought it would help, I would've reassured Sophie that she had nothing to worry about. Based on her mood, I was certain saying anything would only make the situation worse.

"It's a personal matter, and none of..." Shawna said. I could tell she'd had enough of Sophie's brusque attitude and was preparing to deliver some of her own.

"It's regarding some of Roger Nelson's artwork," I interrupted. As much as I appreciated my friend's protective nature, having them get into an argument wasn't going to help our cause.

Sophie jerked her attention from Shawna to me. "Roger was a nice man. He…" Her furrowed brows deepened, and she jutted her chin toward the side of the house. "You'll find Amos down on the beach."

Sophie's demeanor seemed to have gotten worse. She'd been in a disagreeable state since our arrival, so it was hard to tell if mentioning Roger was what had irritated her even more. And if it had, I definitely wanted to know why.

After staring at the slammed door for a few seconds, Jade finally said, "Okay then, I guess we're headed for the beach."

Roger had been standing off to the side with his hands tucked in his coat pockets and intently listening to our conversation. As soon as my friends and I left the porch, he fell in step beside me.

"Was it me, or did Sophie seem a bit obsessed when it came to discussing her husband?" Shawna asked. She nervously glanced back at the house as if expecting Sophie to pop back outside and eavesdrop on our conversation.

"I picked up on that as well," Jade said.

"Roger, do you have any idea what's going on with Sophie?" I asked. "Did she act like that when you knew her before?"

"Most of the time, she was a pleasant person to be around but seemed a little high-strung when she caught Amos flirting with any of the female students," Roger said. "I always thought his friendly behavior was harmless, a way to encourage more business, but maybe I was mistaken. Maybe something was going on that I didn't know about."

I repeated what he said to my friends.

"You know." Shawna flashed Jade and me a contemplative look. "According to the Universal Whodunit Guide—"

"If the circumstances are right, anyone can commit

murder," Jade finished for her.

"Yes, we know," I added, then giggled when Shawna frowned.

"Fine," Shawna huffed. "All I'm saying is if Roger was a woman, Sophie would be at the top of my suspect list."

I couldn't dispute my friend's reasoning. "Roger, did Sophie know about your treasure?"

"Not that I'm aware of," he said. "I suppose Amos could've said something to her, but I doubt it."

If Sophie didn't know about the treasure, then using the information Shawna derived from the guide was moot. At the moment, I couldn't think of any circumstance that would push Sophie to take Roger's life.

I could never decide if being overly curious was a gift or a curse. Sophie's behavior was troubling, and I knew it would niggle in the back of my mind until I figured out the cause. "Is Sophie also an artist?" I asked.

Roger shook his head. "Sadly, no."

"Did the lack of talent create problems between Amos and her?" I asked, knowing my friends would deduce Roger's half of the conversation from mine.

"Sophie seemed to be okay with it," Roger said. "She took care of the administrative side of things, or at least she used to."

The early morning air was cool, and as soon as we left the protection of the house, a brisk breeze swept in from the ocean. My jacket didn't provide as much protection as I would've liked, and I was glad I'd decided to wear a lightweight sweater underneath.

"Sophie handles the management side of things," I said to Jade and Shawna.

"She must be doing a good job, or they wouldn't be in business anymore," Jade said, pulling the front of her jacket closer to her chest.

"Yeah, maybe," Shawna said, though she didn't sound convinced.

I paused when I reached the end of the lawn and

noticed an embankment too high to easily descend to the beach. It didn't take long to find some wooden steps covered with a light layer of sand and tucked between two embankments sporadically filled with patches of tall grass.

"This way," I said, latching onto the handrail as I descended to the area below with my friends and Roger trailing after me. The beach extended in both directions, but the rock formations bordering both sides of the property provided some privacy from the neighbors. Not that it was something Amos and Sophie had to worry about. The homes along this area of the coast were built a good distance apart.

"I don't see him anywhere, do you?" Shawna asked after doing a complete turn and searching in all directions.

I heard what sounded like a person trying to talk above the ocean waves slapping against the rocks. "Over there," I said and waved at the man who'd appeared carrying a bright orange children's bucket.

"Good morning, ladies," Amos shouted, returning my wave. He'd dressed for the cool weather by donning a thigh-length jacket and water-proof boots that rose above his ankles and covered the bottom portion of his pants.

"I'm Amos," he said, giving us a welcoming smile as he tromped toward us through the moist sand. "Which one of you is Rylee?"

"That would be me," I said, holding out my hand to shake. "And these are my friends Shawna and Jade."

"Nice to meet you all," Amos said. The man was genuinely charming, so it was easy to see why his students liked him. The fact that he was handsome and appeared to be in good shape for a man in his mid-fifties didn't hurt either.

"You'll have to excuse my appearance." Amos swept his free hand along his front. "I was doing a little treasure hunting."

"Treasure?" I asked, sharing a concerned glance with Jade and Shawna. I heard Roger grumble but refrained from glancing in his direction.

"Yes." Amos gripped the bottom of the bucket with his other hand, then tipped it so we could take a look.

I'd been holding my breath and thinking that we'd found our killer until I'd glimpsed inside and seen the white, gray, and coral shells.

"Sophie and I are visiting one of our neighbors later today," Amos said. "Their eight-year-old son loves to come over and search for seashells. He calls them his treasures."

"Aww, that's so sweet," Shawna said.

"I know it's been a few years, but talking about a treasure reminds me of Roger and the map he was so secretive about," Amos said, a melancholy expression passing over his face. "The only reason I'd thought of it was because you'd mentioned an interest in his artwork when you called."

"Did you know Roger used to rent the apartment above my family's shop?" I asked, hoping that giving Amos a little history first would help him open up and share something useful.

Amos widened his hazel eyes. "Spencer... Are you related to Abigail?"

His mention of Grams was the complete opposite of Sophie's. "My grandmother," I said. "Do you know her?"

"Not well. I met her when I volunteered on a town committee years ago." He smiled. "Though I have to admit she is quite a character and hard to forget."

I ignored Roger's laughter and the amused look Shawna and Jade shared with each other. "Yep, that's her all right," I said, glad Grams had left him with a good impression. It was hard to get information from someone when they had an issue with one of your relatives. Most people liked my grandmother, but not everyone found her peculiarities endearing.

"What can I help you with?" Amos asked.

"I own one of Roger's seaside works and thought it

would be nice to have another one to hang in my living room," I said, using the only fabrication I could come up with on short notice. Roger's artwork had a spendy price tag when he was alive and outside my range of budget-minded purchases. I could only imagine what they'd be worth now that he was dead.

It was a good thing Amos hadn't heard Roger's grunt or seen Jade's raised brow; otherwise, he would've figured out that I wasn't being entirely truthful. I'd discovered that helping ghosts sometimes put me in situations that would be handled better by a professional investigator. Since I lacked in that department, I had to make things up as I went along.

Fortunately, Amos didn't know about Roger's spirit or that I was really trying to find his killer and was happy to oblige with my request. "Roger rented one of the small rooms at the school and used it as his private studio," Amos said. "When no one came to claim his artwork, I contacted his sister and got permission to sell them for her."

"Let's head back up to the house." He motioned us toward the stairs. "I believe I have a list of the people who purchased Roger's remaining paintings on my office computer."

"Are you sure Sophie won't mind?" Jade asked, wariness creeping into her voice.

There was a good chance Amos had the same information on a computer at the school. I didn't have a problem making the trip if it meant not having to deal with his irritable wife again.

"She won't mind at all," Amos chuckled. "Why do you ask?"

Either the man was oblivious when it came to his wife's nature, or she acted differently when he was around. "Um, no reason," I said.

As soon as we entered the house, Amos took us down a short hallway from the foyer to his office. Sophie was nowhere in sight, and if our luck held, we wouldn't have to deal with her again before we left.

I gave the room an admiring glance. It was spacious with a large window overlooking the ocean and the beach we'd recently been standing on. The interior walls were done in an off-white, and the room was furnished with a large mahogany desk, a dark leather office chair, and a sofa.

"That's one of Roger's works," Amos said, pointing at a painting hanging on the wall opposite his desk. The beautiful picture depicted a scenic coastline as if painted from the top of a bluff. Three paintings centered with equal spacing between them took up the remaining area on the wall. The brush strokes in the additional artwork were different than Roger's but similar enough to know they were done by the same artist, which I assumed was Amos.

"That's not the painting we're looking for," Roger said, his voice laced with disappointment.

I hadn't been worried about him reverting to his prankster ways while we were outside. There really was much he could move around on the beach. Not unless he decided to scoop up sand and toss it into the air.

Since we were inside the house where he had access to numerous objects, I monitored him with inconspicuous glances. He hadn't actually promised to behave himself, but he'd done a good job so far, and I hoped to keep it that way.

Amos took a seat in the chair next to his desk and started typing on the keyboard. "Oh," he said after perusing the computer screen. "I'd forgotten all about the special finger painting class I was teaching around the same time Roger…" Sadness filled his eyes, and he paused to swallow and gain his composure.

After tapping a few more keys, Amos said, "There were only two finished paintings, and they were purchased by students in the class."

"Do you happen to have their names?" I asked, trying

not to sound too excited.

"Yes, one was Polly Hederman, and the other was Ethan Atwell," Amos said. "Do you know either of them?"

"Polly, most definitely," Shawna said. "We stop by the Tasty Trinkets regularly."

"You wouldn't happen to know where we can find Ethan, do you?" I asked, trying to determine if they had a close relationship and to find out if they'd stayed in contact over the years. When dealing with murder, there was always a chance more than one killer was involved. If so, I didn't want to rule out the possibility until I was sure.

"As a matter of fact, I believe he's working as a mechanic for Hank Harvey," Amos said. He got up from his seat and took a few steps toward the door, a sign that our meeting was coming to an end.

Hank owned the Custom Fender automobile repair shop. Hopefully, being a regular customer for years would come in handy when I talked to Ethan.

"We really appreciate all your help," I said after Amos returned us to the foyer.

"It was my pleasure," Amos said, holding the front door open for us. "You might also want to stop by the new art gallery and talk to Kevin Patterson. He's putting together a display for local artists for viewing during his grand opening. He's already been by and collected several of my paintings."

Kevin had moved to Cumberpatch over the holidays. Unfortunately, our initial meeting had been a result of his Aunt Evelyn's death. He and Jade had hit it off immediately. Once he'd relocated his gallery and had it up and running, I knew it would only be a matter of time before Jade announced that they were officially dating.

Jade's muffled groan, along with the annoyed look she shot me, was a warning not to devise any plans that involved using her to get Kevin's help. I reciprocated by flashing an I-have-no-idea-what-you're-talking-about smile, then turned to Amos and said, "We might do that, thanks."

CHAPTER EIGHT

The trip to see Amos hadn't been a waste of time. He'd confirmed that Polly and Ethan had each bought one of Roger's paintings after his death. It didn't necessarily mean they'd been after his treasure or knew that one of the paintings contained his hidden clues. It did, however, mean my friends and I were a little closer to helping Roger find his niece's birthday gift, provided someone else hadn't located it first. I continued to hope that finding the treasure would also help us uncover the identity of his killer.

Jade, Shawna, and I arrived at the shop in time to open. Though I was certain Grams wouldn't need our help. "Don't you have to work the lunch hour?" I asked Shawna when she followed Jade and me inside instead of going home to get ready for her shift.

"I do, but I want to hear what Grams has to say about our update."

"Okay then," I said, dropping my purse and my jacket off in the office before heading to the front of the shop.

When we entered the front room, Grams had finished turning the sign on the front door announcing we were open. "Is Roger with you?" she asked as soon as we entered the room. Her tarot reading must have finished because there weren't any customers in the place yet. She wasn't one to let go of a grudge, and after hearing her wary tone, I got the feeling that she was still perturbed with him.

"No," I said.

The instant we'd stepped off Amos's front porch, Roger had disappeared without any warning. I was getting used to having ghosts showing up and taking off unexpectedly, but it would be nice if they'd take the time to say goodbye or let me know where they were heading next.

Grams grinned as she walked around the display case next to the cash register and propped her elbows on the glass counter. "How did it go with Sophie?" she asked.

"She's not exactly someone I'd choose to hang out with," I said, snatching Barley off the floor to keep him away from the herbal bottles. I cuddled him against my chest and scratched his head until he started purring. The noise was comforting and always worked like magic to ease my stress.

"Or meet on a dark street late at night," Jade chuckled.

"Still scary then," Grams said.

"What's the deal with her anyway?" Shawna asked, sidling in next to Grams and tapping her nails on the glass. "The entire time we talked to her, she eyed us as if we'd planned to steal her husband away from her."

"Well." Grams drew out the word, her way of making what she was about share sound mysterious. "According to rumors, a few years back, a student got infatuated with Amos, and they supposedly had a tryst."

"You mean they hooked up, and Amos cheated on Sophie," Shawna said.

"Do you know the name of the student?" Jade asked, then bent forward to stuff her purse on the shelf beneath the cash register.

"Or if Sophie did something to her?" I asked. Given the way she'd acted earlier, and the fact that she and Amos were still together, it was easy to imagine that Sophie had made the student go away.

"No idea," Grams said. "Like I said, it was only a rumor, or…"

"Or what?" Shawna asked.

My grandmother was a pro at luring people in with her tales. Today, the immunity I'd developed over the years wasn't working. I set Barley back on the floor and moved closer to hear what she had to say.

"She used magic to cover it up," Grams said.

"What?" My friends and I exclaimed at the same time.

I was the first to recover my shock and asked, "Why would you think she used magic?"

"I heard Sophie is a distance cousin to one of the witching families in the area," Grams said, tucking several strands of hair behind her ear. "Though I couldn't tell you which one or if she actually practices the art."

"A witch… Seriously Grams," I huffed, thoroughly annoyed with my grandmother. "Don't you think you could have told us that before we made the trip over there?" My friends didn't say anything but were clearly thinking the same thing. Jade pursed her lips, and Shawna shifted sideways to glare at Grams.

"Would it have stopped you from going or trying to find answers to help Roger?" Grams asked.

"Well, no, probably not," I said, shuddering at the thought of having to deal with him daily. Would his ability to move things improve the longer he was in our realm? And, if they did, how bad would his pranks get?

"I told you to take Jade and Shawna with you, didn't I?" Grams pushed away from the counter and placed her hands on her hips. "You might have been fine on your own, but I knew Sophie wouldn't try anything if the three of you showed up together."

After meeting Sophie, I had my doubts and wondered about my grandmother's level of certainty. My thoughts also drifted toward my theory about magic being involved in Roger's death. If Grams was right about Sophie's connections to the magical world, then I couldn't disregard her as a suspect.

When I'd mentioned Roger to her, Sophie had seemed genuinely upset about his death. The emotions she'd displayed gave me conflicting views on whether or not she'd intentionally killed him.

"Since you survived your visit without being hexed, did you find out anything interesting from Amos?" Grams asked. "What did he say when you asked him about Roger's treasure? Did he express any suspicious behaviors?" She went back to leaning on the counter again, eager to hear our juicy tidbits.

I started answering her questions, beginning with the last one first. "No unusual behaviors."

I also told her about finding Amos collecting seashells, his mention of Roger's treasure, and apparent disinterest in the subject. "Amos told us he sold two of Roger's paintings. One to Polly Hederman and the other to Ethan Atwell. One of them could be the painting we're missing."

"Do you need my help doing recon with Polly?" Grams asked.

I stifled a grin after hearing my grandmother use the word she'd picked up from Shawna.

"No, we're good," I told her.

Jade, Shawna, and I had already discussed visiting the Tasty Trinkets after work. We planned to use eating out as a way to question Polly. Since it was the weekend, and Polly was the owner, chances were good that she'd be there.

Grams frowned at my response, turning my amusement into concern that she might arrange a covert mission of her own. "Besides, it's Saturday," I said. "Don't you have plans to do something with Mattie?"

"I do, but if you need our help, I'm sure Mattie won't mind a diversion," Grams said.

"Thanks for the offer, but I think we've got it

covered," I said, glancing at my friends for support and receiving confirming noises.

"Okay, then what about that Ethan fellow?" Grams asked.

"Also taken care of," I said. "And if it's all right with you, I need to make a trip to Hank's shop this afternoon."

Grams pushed away from the counter. "Why? Is something wrong with your car?"

Keeping my vehicle maintained and drivable was something my grandmother stressed even before I'd gotten my license. "No," I said before she gave me the lecture I'd heard many times before. "Amos told us that Ethan works for Hank. I figured taking my car in was the best way to chat with him about Roger's painting."

Jade furrowed her brows and crossed her arms. "Sure, because discussing mechanical issues is a great way to transition into talking about art." Her sarcastic tone was laced with worry.

"Remember what Roger said about Ethan taking his class," Shawna said. "If he's an artist, then maybe Jade's new boyfriend will have one of his paintings displayed at the gallery. Just find a way to work the grand opening into your conversation."

"Kevin is not my boyfriend," Jade snapped. "We haven't even been on a date."

"But you have been talking on the phone and texting each other," Shawna said, grinning when Jade scowled at her.

"Do you want someone to go with you?" Grams asked, still unwilling to be excluded.

At some point today, Roger would reappear. Having a ghost who could move objects tagging along wasn't as risky as a grandmother with a tendency to cause turmoil. "No, it's going to get busy soon, and I'm sure I'll be safe with Hank hanging around." I narrowed my gaze. "Unless you think he has some mystical powers I don't know about."

Hank had to be one of the easiest-going people I knew, and it would take a lot of convincing for me to believe he had a connection with anything paranormal.

Grams tsked. "The only magic that man knows how to wield is under the hood of a car."

"That's for sure," Shawna chuckled.

"Have you heard back from Bryce yet?" Jade asked

I adored my friend for noticing my frustration and shifting the conversation in a different direction. "Not yet," I said, puffing out a breath. I'd hoped that discovering what caused Roger to change into a poltergeist would also help us locate his killer.

The bell above the door jingled, announcing a visitor and putting an end to any further speculations about our ghostly investigation. The display case we were all gathered around was the only place in the shop with a direct line of sight to the front door. We all turned to see Logan saunter into the shop. His brown hair, a silky shade of dark chocolate, laid in perfect layers. The cut was short, but the lengths along his nape lightly brushed the collar of his tan suede jacket.

"Ladies," he said, addressing all of us, but the smile on his handsome face was directed solely at me.

I smiled back, wondering if there'd ever come a time when my stomach didn't experience rapid butterfly wing movements at the sight of him.

"Good morning, Logan," Jade, Shawna, and Grams chimed.

My cat had his favorites when it came to people, and Logan was near the top of the list. As soon as Barley heard his voice, he appeared from wherever he'd been hiding so he could rub against Logan's leg. With a chuckle, Logan picked Barley up off the floor. He was well aware of the routine and knew that he'd risk having tiny claws latch onto his pant leg if he ignored my cat.

After plying Barley with the appropriate amount of attention, Logan set him back on the floor, then scrutinized our group with his dark whiskey gaze. "I'm not interrupting something, am I?"

Other than a few nervous giggles, none of us answered. Logan was good at his job, and it wouldn't take him long to figure out we were hiding something from him. Even less time for one of us to tell him what he wanted to know.

Shawna, being the only one who could escape, said, "I should probably get going, or I'll be late for work." She didn't wait for a reply as she stepped from behind the counter. Instead of walking past Logan to leave through the front, she took the hallway to the back of the building and the small lot where she'd parked her car next to mine.

Shawna wasn't an employee, but since she was practically family, she'd earned access rights to all the other parts of the shop.

"It looks like you're going to have to tell Logan about Roger sooner than you expected," Jade whispered before moving to an adjoining aisle and pretending to straighten candles on one of the shelves.

My friends were supportive when faced with adversity. Or at least adversity that wasn't in the form of the perceptive detective walking toward me.

Grams, on the other hand, stayed where she was so she could overhear our conversation.

"Grams. Do you mind?" I asked, then urged her to give us some privacy by tipping my head.

"Fine," she harrumphed, then went to join Jade.

"Hey," I said, rising up on my toes to give Logan a hug. "I thought you had to work today. What brings you by the shop?"

"I had some police business in the area and thought I'd stop by and see if you were free to get some coffee." His wide smile showed off his dimples. "And maybe one of Mattie's decadent desserts."

We shared the love of sweets, though, for me, it was a weakness that could easily be exploited. Not that I thought Logan had suggested it to pry information out of me.

"I can definitely make the time if there's going to be dessert involved," I said with a wink.

"What about spending time with me?" he asked with a teasing pout.

"I suppose that would be a bonus." I followed him back down the aisle, pausing to give Grams and Jade a goodbye wave. Once outside, Logan offered me his arm and led me toward the crosswalk that would take us across the street to Mattie's place.

While we waited for traffic to pass and the light to change, I contemplated how I would explain Roger's appearance to Logan. He might support my ability, but he was never happy when my friends and I decided to investigate the departed's murders. It was one of those things we hadn't quite figured out yet. Besides, if it turned out that Roger really had been murdered, once my friends and I had proof, we'd need the help of local law enforcement.

When the pedestrian sign signaled it was safe for us to go, I stepped into the street mentally selecting the details I wanted to share and secretly hoping I'd be able to enjoy my spontaneous date without any ghostly interference.

CHAPTER NINE

Mattie's place was well-known for its wide selection of coffees and baked breakfast items. She even served delicious sandwiches for lunch. No other place in Cumberpatch compared when it came to her delicious desserts, most of which oozed with chocolate, caramel, or some type of fruit.

Any time of the day worked fine for me when it came to indulging in sweets. Mid-morning happened to be the best time to stop by Mattie's. The breakfast rush was over, and the people occupying tables were either tourists or a handful of locals who worked later shifts.

"Morning," Mattie called to us when the bell that closely resembled the one in our shop jingled.

Trina, Mattie's employee, who was helping a customer at the opposite end of the counter, smiled and waved. She'd started out as a part-time worker until she'd finished high school, then got promoted to full-time and worked the morning and lunchtime shifts. Her ponytail swung back and forth as she moved between the coffee machine and the display case filled with all the goodies they offered.

"Hey, Mattie," I said as I stepped inside the shop.

"How are things going?" she asked when we'd reached

the area along the long counter designated for ordering by a large sign hanging from the ceiling.

Her inquisitive tone held an additional ounce of curiosity, more than I'd expect from a casual inquiry. Grams and Mattie were best friends and shared everything. Mattie never said anything about my unique abilities, but of the small circle privy to the information, I knew Grams had included her. I'd be surprised if she hadn't already received an update from Grams via text about our investigation into Roger's murder.

Logan didn't remark on Mattie's comment, but the subtle raising of one brow was a good indication he hadn't missed the underlying subtext of her question either.

"Everything looks good today," I said, anxious to change the subject. I dropped my gaze to peruse the yummy items lining the shelves on the other side of the glass.

Mattie was quick to catch on. "Do you two want your usual, or are you going for something new?"

My usual was a large brownie covered with hot fudge and caramel, heavier on the topping than depicted in the picture on Mattie's menu. "Yes, please, with a black coffee," I said, glancing at Logan to see if he was going to try something different.

"Make mine the same," he said, reaching for his wallet. "Why don't you find us a place to sit?"

I didn't want our conversation to be overheard, so I grabbed a table near the front window. The location was far enough away from other customers and ensured we'd have some privacy.

Logan followed me to the table a few minutes later, carrying a tray with our order.

"Thanks," I said, eagerly reaching for a fork after he'd set one of the plates and a coffee down in front of me.

"How have you been?" he asked after placing the tray on the empty table next to us.

Because of his job and the increase in tourist traffic,

work had kept him busy, and we hadn't seen each other for two days. Until he'd relocated to Cumberpatch, handling cases that involved homicides had been his priority. Now, his daily assignments included dealing with all types of crimes, something he seemed to enjoy.

For once, I was glad that we'd been using texts to communicate, that he hadn't had a chance to call. If Logan had heard my voice, he'd have known I was up to something, and I wouldn't have been able to prolong telling him about Roger and my newest sleuthing adventure. I'd hoped by the time we finally talked that I'd have something more tangible to tell him.

When my ghosts accompanied an actual body, and the victim was one of Logan's cases, it made things less complicated. Some of the investigating my friends and I did pushed the boundaries of legal, but things had a way of working themselves out...most of the time.

"I've been good," I said, scooping a large piece of brownie up with my fork. "Keeping busy with the shop." After stuffing the morsel in my mouth and enjoying its delectable goodness, I raised my gaze to see him staring at me over the rim of his cup.

I couldn't tell if the amusement sparkling in his eyes was from watching me eat or if he knew I was stalling to avoid telling him what I'd really been doing. I decided to go with the latter.

Until recently, the most assistance Logan provided was lecturing me on the dangers of dealing with killers and how I shouldn't get involved.

After enlightening him about being able to see ghosts, things had changed. Because I could end up being haunted forever if I didn't help them find their hereafter, not getting involved wasn't an option. Even so, I didn't want to abuse our relationship by asking for his help. I rationalized that explaining the murder aspects of Roger's situation in theoretical terms wasn't really asking, only obtaining a professional opinion.

"Let's say, hypothetically, that I recently had an encounter with one of my special visitors," I said. "And this guest mentioned an unusual situation...a situation that fringes on your area of expertise."

Logan stopped the fork holding his next bite of brownie inches from his mouth. "Can you be more specific, hypothetically speaking?"

I nodded as I glanced around to make sure I hadn't drawn anyone's attention before continuing, "Let's say that summoning this particular visitor was an accident. He didn't come with a body, and his death was reported as natural causes several years ago, but there's a possibility it was something different."

Logan set the fork back on his plate, leaned back in his chair, crossed his arms, and gave me his full attention. I was certain if I could read his thoughts, which thankfully I couldn't, I'd have heard him say "this ought to be good." Instead, his voice switched from boyfriend to detective mode. "Rylee, what's really going on?"

"Do you remember me telling you about Roger Nelson?" I reached for my cup, then blew on the hot liquid before taking a sip.

"Wasn't he the person who rented your apartment from your parents before you moved in?" Logan asked. "The one who did the painting hanging on the wall behind your couch."

"That's him," I said, touched that he remembered small details about the things I shared with him. Some of the guys I'd dated in the past, not that there'd been more than a handful, weren't nearly as attentive and rarely showed an interest in things I enjoyed discussing.

"Why do you ask?"

I leaned forward and lowered my voice, then explained how Barley's playful antics with the picture frame had led to me being haunted by Roger.

"Didn't he die from a heart attack?" Logan asked, his voice laced with intrigue. "That's the natural causes you were talking about, correct?"

"Yes, supposedly," I said, then went on to tell him about Roger being able to move objects.

"Is that a new development?" Logan asked. "I don't remember you mentioning it before."

"Yeah, one I'm still trying to figure out," I said, not sure if I was ready to share my theory about magic being the source of Roger's ability.

"I take it you already talked to Bryce about it."

I smiled at how well Logan knew me. "I did, but he couldn't find much information, other than speculating that Roger might be a poltergeist."

"Interesting," he said, rubbing his chin. "When you mentioned fringing on my area of expertise, were you implying that you think he was murdered?" Logan kept his voice low and glanced around the same way I had.

Several tables had emptied since we'd arrived. Two were still occupied. One by a man focused on reading his newspaper and the other by a mother busy managing her overactive children. I didn't want to point out that giving them sweets this early in the day might not have been a wise decision.

"Not me specifically," I said. "It was more Roger's theory than mine. Though I do agree since he's still here and has some unfinished business."

"Isn't an unnatural death usually the unfinished business?" Logan asked, then picked up his fork and stuffed the brownie in his mouth.

"As far as I know, it is, but in Roger's case, there's an additional task he's asked me to complete before he can move on to the afterlife."

"What kind of task?" Curiosity with a touch of concern flickered in Logan's eyes.

"I'm afraid I can't say."

Logan frowned. "Why not?"

I shrugged. "I sort of promised Roger I wouldn't tell anyone else."

"You mean anyone else other than Jade and Shawna," he said unhappily and sounding hurt.

"And Grams," I added sheepishly. There was no point in hiding her involvement. He'd already witnessed our huddle at the shop, so it wouldn't take him long to make the connection.

"I really wish I could tell you, but…" The empty chair situated between Logan and me scraped the floor as it moved away from the table and ended my apologetic explanation. So did the appearance of Roger's translucent form as he took a seat.

I quickly scooted my chair towards his, hoping the others in the room would think I was responsible for moving the chair and making the disruptive noise. I was impressed at how well Logan handled the interruption. His flinch was barely noticeable and nothing like Nate's dramatic display when he'd first found out about Martin. The situation had been similar; only Nate had literally jumped away from the table at the restaurant.

I'm sure recently learning that Roger could move objects had helped minimize Logan's reaction.

The woman with the children had been herding them toward the exit. If she'd noticed the disruption, it hadn't registered as something interesting. The man sitting by himself glared at us, gave the newspaper a hard shake, then went back to reading.

Trina and Mattie hadn't seemed to notice either. They were busy behind the counter prepping for the lunch crowd due to begin arriving in another hour.

"Roger," I said, acting as if I was speaking to Logan while glimpsing the ghost. "What are you doing here?"

"I came for an update," Roger said, crossing his arms as he leaned back in his chair. "I didn't expect to find you on a date."

It was hard to take his admonishment seriously when the blue smock he wore was covered with cute little cats wearing artist berets. "Can't your update wait until *later*?" I asked, cluing Logan in on Roger's request.

Roger ignored my question because he was too busy giving Logan a once-over. "He does appear to be an improvement over that other guy you were dating."

I was surprised that Roger remembered Hudson Bradley, my ex-boyfriend, who'd thankfully moved to Portland not long after I discovered he was cheating on me.

Logan was definitely an improvement in every way, even when he used his intense detective stare, which at times, could be unnerving. "You'll be glad to know my friend approves of my choice in boyfriends," I said to Logan.

"He does, does he?" Logan asked, then grinned.

"Yes, and in case you didn't know, I wholeheartedly agree," I said, earning me an even bigger smile. Embarrassing the man was hard to do, yet my compliment had a dash of red blossoming on Logan's cheeks.

"Before you go," I said to Roger, reminding him that he still needed to leave. "Would you mind if I told Logan about the project you asked me to keep a secret?" Trying not to divulge too much, I chose my next words carefully. "He's very trustworthy and might be able to help find that person you're looking for." The person being Roger's niece.

Roger made a contemplative sound and straightened in his seat. "I guess it would be all right," he said, then disappeared without so much as a goodbye.

"My friend left, but he said to tell you—"

Logan's cell phone rang, and he quickly slipped it out of his jacket pocket. "This is Detective Prescott," he said, pausing to listen to whoever was on the other end of the call. "Are you sure?" he groaned, swiping a hand through his hair. "I'll be there as soon as I can." He disconnected the call, then got to his feet.

"I take it you have to go," I said.

"Sorry, but yeah." He stepped around the chair Roger

had occupied to reach me. After tipping up my chin, he brushed a kiss across my lips. "I'll call you later so we can finish our conversation." He took a step, then stopped and narrowed his dark whiskey eyes. "Please don't do anything that will put you in harm's way."

CHAPTER TEN

After Logan rushed from Mattie's shop to deal with whatever law enforcement business he'd been summoned to, I finished the last few bites of my brownie and pondered his departing remark. He hadn't told me *not* to do anything regarding Roger's murder, nor did he lecture me on the dangers of doing my own investigating. It was progress, and I looked forward to spending more time with him, even if it was to discuss Roger.

Once I'd tossed the paper plates and cups in the nearest waste receptacle and placed the tray on a stack with several others, I waved at Trina and Mattie, then headed back to the shop.

As soon as I stepped inside, I spotted Grams standing near a display in the area I'd dubbed dark and ominous because of all the paranormal products lining the shelves. My father took pride in keeping his favorite section stocked with items I sometimes thought were questionable. She was showing two women our limited collection of books on magical lore. Their oohs and awes were a good indication that my grandmother had guaranteed more sales.

I moved toward the back of the room where Jade was

working. "What happened to Logan," she asked. After opening a box she'd placed on the counter, she pulled out several stacks of plastic bags stamped with the shop's logo and set them on a shelf underneath.

"He got called away on an emergency," I said.

"That's too bad." Jade wrinkled her nose. "How did the rest of your date go?"

"Fine until Roger showed up and wanted an update on our progress." I walked around the counter to stand next to her.

"It's only been a few hours since he went with us to see Amos." Jade retrieved another stack. "Did he really think we'd be able to find more clues in such a short time?"

"Personally, I think he's lonely. I can't imagine how awful it must have been to be trapped in the park with no one to talk to for such a long time."

"You're probably right," Jade said, pulling the last of the bags out of the box. "Did he show up before or after Logan left?"

"Right before," I said.

Jade glanced across the shop to make sure Grams was still helping her customer. "Did you get a chance to tell him about Roger's demise theories?"

"I got as far as sharing what we'd learned from Bryce, not about the investigating we've been doing?"

"How about the other thing?" Jade asked.

I knew she was referring to Roger's treasure. "I told him I was helping with unfinished business but couldn't tell him what it was."

"I'll bet that went well with Mr. Hotty Detective," Jade chuckled.

"He wasn't too happy about it, not after he figured out that Shawna, Grams, and you all know."

"I'm sorry." Jade's pout didn't seem all that sympathetic.

"It's fine," I said. "Roger gave me permission to tell Logan about the *other thing* the next time I see him."

Footsteps alerted me that Grams and the two women she'd been helping were heading toward us. I picked up the empty box. "I'll drop this off in the back on my way out."

When I didn't supply Jade with any more information, she asked, "You're still planning to visit Hank's place, right?"

"Yeah. Maybe I'll get lucky and uncover a clue that will lead us to the missing painting or Roger's...you know." I didn't want to say killer and chance being overheard by our customers.

"Even so,"—Jade placed her hand on my arm—"you need to be careful and call if you run into trouble."

I glanced across the store where my grandmother had stopped to point out a shelf filled with souvenirs. "I will and let Grams know I should be back in an hour, two at the latest."

CHAPTER ELEVEN

I spent most of the drive to the Custom Fender trying to figure out the best way to get Ethan to show me the painting he'd purchased from Amos, provided he still owned it. I also needed to find out if he'd been interested in Roger's treasure and been responsible for his death.

It wasn't like I could walk into Hank's place and immediately start asking about something that had happened years ago. Not without getting weird looks or putting people on the defensive. It hadn't taken me long to realize that gathering clues was a lot easier when the ghost in question belonged to a recently deceased person.

When I stopped a block away from the auto repair shop, patiently waiting for the light to change from red to green, cold air flooded the inside of my car. "Where are you going now?" Roger asked as he appeared in the passenger seat. The cute smock I've seen earlier was gone, but the beret had remained.

One of these days, preferably before I had my own heart attack, I was going to remember to ask Joyce and Edith if there was such a thing as a magical bell I could have the ghosts wear so they didn't startle me every time they appeared.

"Do you remember Amos telling us that Ethan worked for Hank?" The light changed, and I pressed on the accelerator. Hank's shop had been around for a long time. He had a stellar reputation for auto repair, so I assumed Roger must have been a customer since he didn't act surprised when I mentioned Hank's name.

"And you're certain Amos was telling the truth, that Ethan is working there now?" Roger asked.

"Not really, but I couldn't call ahead to check without sounding too conspicuous," I said, making a right into the shop's parking lot. "If Ethan is the killer, we don't want to tip him off."

"Good point," Roger said, then smiled. "You're better at this sleuthing thing than I thought."

"Thanks." Roger giving me or anyone else a compliment was rare, but it had my cheeks heating nonetheless.

After finding a place to park, I shifted sideways to give Roger my full attention. "Before we go inside, I want you to promise me that you will not touch or move things around." I didn't care that I was starting to sound like an overbearing mother with a child every time we visited a new place. I was sure Hank had many sharp, pointy tools, and I didn't want anyone to accidentally get hurt if Roger decided to pull one of his pranks. I also didn't need any more witnessed accounts supporting the rumors Lavender had started about me being a witch.

"What if someone threatens your life?" Roger asked.

There was a softer side to him that I hadn't known existed. A side that seemed to slip out more frequently the more time we spent together. "I don't think it's something we have to worry about, but yes, if somebody tries to hurt me, then you have my permission to help."

Satisfied with my answer, Roger exited the vehicle. I was glad he moved through the door rather than moving it. If someone had been passing by on the sidewalk and saw the door open and close by itself, explaining what they'd seen would've been awkward.

When I entered the reception area, Hank was standing behind a long counter, wearing a pair of gray coveralls, his short dark hair slicked back from his face. His gaze went back and forth between a computer keyboard and the screen as he tapped the keys with his index fingers.

Unlike the shops in the main part of town, his door had a buzzer instead of a bell. As soon as the musical time echoed through the room, he looked up from his screen. "Hi Rylee," he said, his smile faltering. "Is there a problem with your car? I don't think you're due for an oil change or maintenance for another month."

"Really?" I asked, nervously adjusting the strap of my purse. "I could've sworn I needed to get it in sooner."

"I can check if you like," Hank said, already reaching for his keyboard.

Sitting on the counter, I noticed a colorful flyer with Kevin's new place, the Cumberpatch Gallery of Fine Arts, printed in bold yellow letters across the top. "Hey, where did you get this?" I asked, snatching the pamphlet and hoping to distract him.

Roger stood quietly near the front door and walked over to look at the flyer over my shoulder. His chilly presence made me glad I hadn't taken off my jacket. If Hank had noticed the sudden drop in temperature, he didn't say anything.

I wondered why Kevin hadn't brought any of the pamphlets by the shop. I would've gladly handed them out to customers to help promote his event. I glanced at the inside of the folded paper and noticed a listing for Amos's school along with contact information for classes. Maybe the flyer was a collaborative promotion and only being handed out to artists and potential students.

"Ethan's a pretty good painter, and he brought it in," Hank said, pointing at the man entering the room through the doorway leading into the repair bays. "I'm not much for the artsy stuff myself."

I'd known Hank a long time, and even if he hadn't said anything, I could've guessed he wasn't an art connoisseur. The only picture he had hanging on the wall was a cute Labrador photo attached to a calendar.

Ethan was younger than I'd expected and looked to be in his late twenties, which meant he hadn't been out of high school long before he'd taken the class with Roger. He was dressed in the same coveralls as Hank, only his were a darker gray and smudged with oil spots. He had a tall, muscular build and sandy blond hair cropped short and off his collar.

He strolled into the room, wiping his greasy hands on a red utility cloth.

"Ethan, this is Rylee Spencer," Hank said.

"Nice to meet ya," Ethan said with a smile.

"Her family owns the Mysterious Baubles."

"That's one of those shops down on Swashbuckler, right?" Ethan asked.

"It is," I said.

"I don't do much shopping, so I'm afraid I've never been."

My family's place was popular, more so with the tourists. Even so, not all the locals had an interest in visiting the place. "That's okay," I said in a reassuring voice. "I'm not a big shopper either." Because of Jade and Shawna's love of checking out new places, I was pretty sure they'd dragged me to every business in Cumberpatch at least once.

I still needed to ask about Roger's painting and directed the conversation back to discussing art by holding up the flyer. "So, Hank tells me you're an artist."

"Uh-huh," Ethan said. "I dabble some, even take a class now and then at the art school." He tucked the dirty cloth in his back pocket. "Amos, the owner, is also a good instructor. I've learned a lot from him."

"That's great," I said, showing ignorance. I didn't know how Ethan would react if I told him I knew Amos and had met with him earlier. He seemed comfortable talking about the school, and I didn't want to risk changing it. "Oh, did you know Roger Nelson before he passed away?" I tried to keep my question as matter-of-fact as possible and added, "He used to rent the apartment above my family's shop, and I believe he also kept a room at the school that he used as a workshop."

"Yep. We took a class together, but that was a long time ago, and I can't say I knew him all that well," Ethan said. "He was a talented artist, though, and I did buy one of his paintings after he died."

"You did?" I asked, pretending I hadn't already gotten the same information from Amos. "I own one of his paintings as well. Would you mind letting me see yours sometime?" Soon would be good, but I didn't want to push him.

"I would except I loaned it to Kevin for his opening." Ethan tapped the flyer I was holding. "It will be on display if you want to go and check it out."

"I'll think about it, thanks," I said, happy I finally had a lead worth following.

I stared at the floor and acted as if I recalled a memory before looking up at Ethan. "Roger used to tell my friends and me that he had a map of a buried treasure," I said. "Did he ever say anything about it to you?" Veering toward a new topic too quickly was risky, but I had to know how much Ethan knew and couldn't think of any other way to bring it up.

I relied on Hank's presence to persuade Ethan to tell the truth, or at least a modified version of what really happened. When you lived in a small community, fabricating information had a way of eventually catching up with you. The odds were in my favor that Ethan didn't want his boss to think badly of him.

Roger had moved into my periphery and was shifting back and forth on his feet, making incoherent grumbling noises. If I could've talked to him, I would've pointed out that I hadn't actually broken my promise not to tell anyone about his treasure, only skirted around the edges a little bit.

"I remember Roger saying something about a treasure. He might have even teased that it belonged to Martin Cumberpatch," Ethan said. "I don't think he really had a map though. 'Cuz if he did, I never found...I mean saw it."

Had Ethan just confessed to being the one who'd gone through Roger's belongings? If he couldn't find the map, what reason would he have for doing away with Roger? No one knew about the clues, so why buy one of his paintings?

Either Ethan thought it would be a good investment, or Amos told him the money from the sale would go to Roger's sister. Had the purchase stemmed from guilt or respect for the older artist?

The more I questioned people, the more confusing and complicated the situation seemed to get.

"Maybe you should get back to work," Hank said to Ethan, pulling me from my thoughts.

I wasn't happy about the interruption, but I couldn't blame Hank. He was running a business, and it wasn't profitable to pay employees for standing around. Even if they were chatting with customers.

"Sure." Ethan stepped behind the counter where Hank was standing to pull a small orange box containing a part from one of the shelves.

Once Ethan left the room, Hank returned to his computer and began tapping keys again. While he stared at the screen, I stuffed the flyer in my pocket. The information on the pamphlet might come in handy later.

"Looks like I was right." Hank grinned, proud of his memory. "You're not due for an oil change until the middle of next month."

"Thanks so much for checking," I said. "I'll make a note and call to set up an appointment later."

"I look forward to hearing from you," he said.

I headed for the door, feeling bad about deceiving Hank and allowing him to go through the trouble of confirming my car's status.

Roger had disappeared before I left the shop, so I was surprised to see him reappear in the passenger seat. "I think that was a productive visit, don't you?" he asked.

"It was helpful," I muttered. I was frustrated that we weren't making much headway and quickly running out of suspects to question. I hadn't gleaned any new clues or gotten a look at the painting that Ethan owned. On the upside, I'd found out where it was going to be and when.

"Do we think Ethan is the person we're searching for?" Roger sounded as unconvinced as I felt.

"I don't think we can omit him quite yet," I said, pulling onto the street that would take us back to Mysterious Baubles. Roger stayed in the car but remained silent for the remainder of the trip. He stared out the window, either noting how the town had changed since his death or, like me, was trying to figure out what we should do next.

CHAPTER TWELVE

Polly was usually working any time my friends and I decided to visit the Tasty Trinkets. I looked forward to eating out but didn't want it to be a wasted trip and called to confirm that she'd be there. Luckily, I'd talked to one of Polly's staff and didn't have to explain to her personally why I wanted to see her.

Lots of places in Cumberpatch were decorated with pirate themes, including the cafe. Polished wooden boards lined most of the walls. A ship's wheel was mounted to the front of the counter that held the cash register and served as a receptionist's welcoming station.

The walls were lined with all kinds of pirate paraphernalia, including various types of sabers and cutlasses. Polly had even mounted a black flag imprinted with a skull and crossbones. I wasn't an expert, but some of the artifacts looked authentic. Several masts, the sails rolled and held in place with thick rope, were mounted to the ceiling. A seascape mural containing a pirate ship had been painted on the wall surrounding the food serving window.

The handful of servers, both men and women, wore uniforms in line with the interior's decor. They all wore vests that cinched up the middle over white shirts for the guys and blouses with short puffy sleeves for the girls. Black pants with comfortable boots completed the ensembles for the male staff.

Polly catered to customers of all ages and had the outfits designed with families in mind. The skirts she'd selected for the girls all had a moderate length, unlike some of the costumes I'd seen at our annual pirate festival, where the hemlines were considerably shorter.

The cafe wasn't far from the park, and Jade, Shawna, and I'd been seated at a booth by the window overlooking an area where people took their dogs to walk and play. We'd left right after closing the shop, giving us plenty of sunlight to watch the activities. With the weather growing steadily warmer, some of the townsfolk were spending more time outside.

Since Logan had helped fill my quota of sweets for the day, I'd already decided on a specialty salad, and after a quick perusal to make sure I didn't want to change my mind, I closed my menu.

The drive to Polly's place took less than ten minutes, so we'd waited to talk about what I'd learned during my visit to Hank's until after we'd placed our orders.

The cafe was already busy, and being that it was Saturday, it wouldn't be long before more people arrived to fill the few remaining empty tables. Anything I said would be muffled by the low rumble from all the conversations going on around us. Even so, gossip was a favorite pastime for many locals, so I chose my words carefully. "My *friend* was right about someone going through his things." I spent the next few minutes filling Jade and Shawna in on what I'd learned from talking to Ethan.

"If Ethan was nosing around looking for the map, then I say we leave him on our list," Shawna said.

"Do you think he's the one responsible for...the event?" Jade asked, avoiding any mention of Roger's demise.

After dealing with customers all the time, some more difficult than others, I'd developed an intuitive sense, or as Shawna would say, gotten good at reading vibes. "Unless he's competent at disguising his emotions, I don't think he did it. And neither does my friend."

Becky, our waitress, approached us, balancing a large tray containing our order. She set it on the stand she'd placed near table a few minutes earlier on her way back to the serving window. "Here we go," she said in a pleasant voice as she set plates filled with food down in front of each of us.

"Can I get you anything else?" She tucked the tray under her arm and grabbed the stand.

"No, this looks great, thanks," Jade said, eying her fish platter and draping a napkin over her lap.

"Not for me," I said, reaching for the small dish containing ranch dressing.

"Me either," Shawna said.

"Enjoy." Becky rushed off to help other customers.

I caught a glimpse of Polly flitting about in the kitchen. She liked to interact with her customers, primarily those who lived in Cumberpatch, and would eventually make her way out onto the floor. In the meantime, I planned to enjoy my meal and spend some quality time catching up with my friends.

Though I was curious, I hadn't gotten around to asking Roger where he went whenever he disappeared. He hadn't shown up yet for our latest recon mission, so I thought it was safe to bring up everyday personal items.

Shawna had a metabolism most women would kill for, yet she hadn't attacked her fries and hamburger with her usual vigor. After a few bites of my salad and sharing a concerned look with Jade, I asked, "Are you going out with Nate when we're done here?" If I was wrong about the state of their relationship, I didn't want to come right out and ask if they'd broken things off.

She stared at her plate and answered with a shake of her head.

Jade was better at consoling than I was and reached over to touch Shawna's arm. "Is everything okay between the two of you?"

Shawna released a dejected sigh, then met our worried gazes. "I think he might be cheating on me."

Jade gasped. "No way. I don't believe it. He's crazy about you."

"I agree," I said. "Nate's more into you than any other guy you've ever dated." I knew from experience what that particular betrayal felt like. I hoped my friend was wrong, and we wouldn't be making a trip to the Classic Broom in search of a revenge potion like we had when we were younger after the first guy Shawna had gotten serious about broke her heart.

"I thought so too," Shawna said. She absently dipped a fry in the mound of ketchup she'd squirted on her plate. "But lately, he's been preoccupied and acting secretive." She looked at Jade and me, then forced a half-smile. "Anyway, can we talk about something else?"

"Sure," I said, then noticed Polly heading in our direction, occasionally stopping to greet customers along the way.

I'd gotten in another bite of my salad before she finally reached our table. "Hey," Polly said. "How are you all doing tonight?"

Her light brown hair was pulled back in a stylish braid, and her outfit, an emerald green shirt and black pants, made her stand out from her uniformed staff.

"Fine," I said. Now that I'd gotten some practice with other suspects, I felt more prepared to extract information from Polly. "We were discussing the grand opening at the new art gallery and whether or not we should go." My comment was a little premature since we hadn't exactly talked about attending yet, and earned me an inquisitive look from Jade and a furrowed brow from Shawna.

"You absolutely should," Polly said, straightening her shoulders. "One of my paintings is going to be on display." She tucked a loose strand behind her ear.

"I didn't know you painted," Jade said, her fib sounding even better than mine.

"Nowadays, I do it to relax," Polly chuckled. "That is when and if I can manage to take a day off."

"So if we go, we'll be able to see some of your work?" I asked.

"No, the painting I loaned the gallery was one I'd purchased and was done by another, more famous artist," Polly said.

"Really? Who?" I asked, even though I already knew the answer.

"Do you remember Roger Nelson?" she asked.

"I do." I nodded. "He used to live in the apartment above my family's shop before he passed away." I couldn't think of any other way to find out about Polly's time at the art school, so I added, "I think Amos and Sophie Newsam let him rent a room for his workshop."

I pretended not to notice Polly's shudder or her paling face when she said, "They did."

"Since you paint, have you ever taken any of their classes?" Jade asked.

"Once, but it was a long time ago." Polly tapped her thigh and glanced around as if trying to find a way to escape. "Well, anyway, Kevin's put together a nice exhibit, so you should check it out. Maybe I'll see you there." She hastened away from our table before I could say anything else.

With the paintings and pretty much everyone I'd questioned telling me they were going to be in the same place at the same time, attending the gallery seemed like a smart thing to do. I reached into the pocket of my jacket, which was lying on the seat next to me, and pulled out the flyer I'd taken from Hank's place. "How do you guys feel about going on another sleuthing expedition?"

CHAPTER THIRTEEN

It turned out that Logan wasn't interested in letting much time pass before getting answers to the questions left unasked at the end of our last date. I'd received a call from him not long after returning home and saying goodbye to Jade and Shawna after our dinner at the Tasty Trinkets.

A knock on my apartment door had me sliding Barley's sleeping form off my lap and placing him in the chair next to the couch before answering. After seeing Logan's smile, I took a few seconds to quell my excitement. "Is this official police business or unofficial boyfriend business?" I asked.

He was still dressed in the outfit he'd been wearing during our semi-date, so he'd more than likely just gotten off work. "A little bit of both," he said, stepping inside and closing the door behind him. He pulled me into his arms. "If you don't mind, I'd like to start with the unofficial part first."

"I don't mind at all." I smiled and slipped my hands over his shoulders. I wasn't looking forward to the official part of our conversation and would've been content to forgo it altogether.

"Wonderful," he said, then gave me one of those long lingering kisses that always left me gasping afterward.

Once my breathing returned to normal, I let him know I was ready for an interrogation by taking his hand and leading him past the kitchen area and into the living room. "So detective, what do you want to know?"

I settled back into the couch's cushions and waited for him to answer. An answer that took longer to receive because my cat insisted on getting his usual cuddle time with Logan first.

"Is your friend here now?" Logan asked, then glanced at the painting on the wall behind us, probably remembering what I'd told him about Roger's arrival.

"Nope, it's only the three of us," I said, giving Barley an extra scratch behind the ears after he'd decided to make himself comfortable on Logan's lap.

"How certain are you that Roger was telling the truth about his death being the result of a murder?" Logan asked, straightening his shoulders as he spoke. It always amazed me at how quickly he shifted his demeanor to fit his roles.

"Not a hundred percent, but pretty close." I gave him the details Roger had given me about the other members in his art class.

"Would I be wrong in assuming that you've already done some investigating of your own?"

"You know I don't have a choice, right?" I asked, prepared to remind him again about the haunting for life thing if I didn't resolve Roger's murder.

He nodded his understanding, then patiently waited for me to answer.

If I was being interrogated by a family member, holding back information wouldn't be a problem. With Logan, not so much. "No, but before you ask, I haven't gone or done anything you might consider unlawful," I said, proud of the fact that helping Roger hadn't crossed any illegal lines. At least not yet.

Logan grinned. "That's good to know."

My cat wasn't happy that Logan had stopped petting him and stretched out his front paws to flex on his leg. After groaning and extracting my cat's claws, he set Barley on the cushion next to him, then shifted his focus to me. "Since there isn't any case associated with Roger's death, there isn't much I can do in a professional capacity," Logan said.

Knowing how meticulous he was about his job, I had no doubt he'd already made an inquiry.

He placed his hand over mine. "It doesn't mean I won't do what I can to help my spirit sleuthing girlfriend and make sure she stays out of harm's way."

Hearing him refer to me as his girlfriend always warmed me from the inside out. Hearing the 'harm's way' part of his statement irked me a little because it really translated into keeping an eye on my friends and me.

"What did Roger say about sharing his unfinished business with me?" Logan asked.

It was cute how he reminded me of a young boy, anxious to be included in a secret. Sometimes my devious nature got the better of me, so I shrugged and, without giving him any details, said, "He's okay with it."

After a few seconds of expectant staring, Logan asked, "Are you going to share?"

"Sure," I giggled, then went on to tell him about Roger's niece, the buried treasure, and how it was possibly tied to his death. "Right now, I'm searching for the other painting so we can put together the clues and see if the treasure is still out there."

"Are you saying you're not trying to figure out who might have killed Roger?" I didn't miss the hint of hope attached to his question.

"Not exactly," I said. "I thought by talking to the people who were in Roger's art class that I might uncover some clues."

"Clues, which I assume, you plan to turn over to me,"

Logan said.

"Of course." I was glad his deduction didn't include a directive.

"Why don't you tell me what you've learned so far," Logan said. "Maybe I can help."

Since I hadn't asked for his assistance, I could still feel good about not personally crossing any relationship boundary lines. I smiled, settled back in the cushions, then started with my trip to see Edwina.

CHAPTER FOURTEEN

Once I'd shared everything I'd learned about my suspects with Logan, it hadn't taken much convincing to get him to attend the Sunday afternoon grand opening at the gallery with me. He couldn't do any official investigating since there was no body, no case, and none of Roger's family had shown up insisting that his death hadn't been an accident. It didn't mean Logan wouldn't put his shrewd detective skills to work by observing all the people I had on my list.

My friends and I had already made plans to go and see if we could find Roger's missing painting. If the artwork wasn't included in the display, then I'd have a bigger problem, like figuring out what else I could do to help the ghost.

Roger was hovering on the sidewalk a few feet from Shawna, Nate, and Jade when we arrived. His body was still a faded translucent blue, but he'd changed his attire to include a nice suit jacket. He'd also switched his artist's beret for a similar one in a dark shade of hunter green.

After making a brief appearance at the shop earlier in the day, he'd asked a few questions about the visit with Polly, then told me he'd see us at the gallery before disappearing. The air held a chilly crispness, so I didn't think anyone was aware of his ghostly presence.

Shawna's concerned disclosure during our meal at the Tasty Trinkets had been unsettling, and I was glad to see her smiling and holding hands with Nate.

Underneath their open jackets, I could see that both of my friends were decked out in dresses. I wasn't surprised that their outfits had been color coordinated to suit their personalities. Jade's black dress was accented with teal accessories, which included her two-inch heels. Shawna had gone with a blue ensemble that matched the streaks in her hair.

I wasn't prone to wearing dresses, but I did own several and had chosen a navy blue one-piece in a simple style that showed off my waist and hips. Seeing the admiring look in Logan's eyes when he'd picked me up, I knew I'd made the right choice.

"Hi guys," I said as soon as we reached them. "And you too, Roger," I added so everyone would know that he was present.

"Have you seen or talked to Kevin yet?" I asked Jade.

"We spoke on the phone when he called to ask if we were still coming," Jade said, her face flushing.

Kevin's initial invite had probably been for Jade. She'd more than likely referred to our group when referencing the call to conceal the fact that she had started pre-dating communications with Kevin from Nate and Logan. She hadn't officially announced the information to Shawna and me either, but my friends and I were close, and I'd noticed the change in her demeanor, the signs that a man had piqued her interest a few weeks ago. Not to mention the hard-to-miss chemistry I'd witnessed the last time we were all gathered in the same place, which happened to be when I'd said goodbye to Kevin's Aunt Evelyn.

"Aren't Bryce and Myra coming?" Logan asked Nate.

The spoofers had a tendency of showing up at local functions together. I hadn't heard back from Bryce yet and was curious to learn if he'd found more information that would enlighten us on Roger's poltergeist situation.

"Myra has a family thing, and Bryce had another commitment. They won't be able to make it," Nate said, his dark brown gaze nervously flitting in my direction as if seeking approval before he divulged any more information. His inquiry was no doubt prompted by Logan's presence and deciding whether or not he should say anything about Bryce's project in front of him.

"Did Bryce happen to mention anything about the research he was doing for me?" I asked.

"Yeah," Nate said. "He told me to tell you he'd call tomorrow."

"Okay, thanks." I was a little disappointed that I'd have to wait another day to find out what Bryce had learned about Roger's situation.

"What project?" Roger asked.

Since he hadn't spoken since Logan and I arrived, I'd almost forgotten he was there. There weren't any other people lingering outside, so talking to Roger directly wasn't a problem. "He's trying to figure out where you got your abilities and if they are linked to your current circumstances." Until I knew more about poltergeists, I wasn't ready to share that we thought he might be one. He didn't seem anxious to move on either, so I didn't want him to consider staying as an option.

"Interesting," Roger said.

Before he could give my answer any more thought, I turned to address the group and found them staring at me. "Why don't we go inside," I said, taking charge and ushering everyone toward the door.

My friends and I had just finished leaving our jackets at the coat check counter near the building's lobby when Grams, along with Mattie and Roy, arrived. Roy, being old-fashioned and a gentleman, at least when he wasn't dealing with criminals, held the door open for the women.

"You all look amazing," Grams said, her gaze bouncing

from one person to the next until she reached Logan. "And you look especially handsome tonight." My grandmother was thrilled that I had a boyfriend. She thought the world of Logan and was determined to make sure he stuck around, which meant taking advantage of every opportunity to practice using her charms on him.

"Thank you, Abigail. You look very nice yourself," Logan said with a wink that had my grandmother blushing like a teenager.

"Grams, please tell me you didn't close the shop," I said, after realizing there was no one left to stay behind and look after the place. The thought of explaining to my parents why we'd lost weekend sales had my stomach knotting.

She tsked and flicked her wrist. "I haven't reached the point of being senile yet. I got your Uncle Max to look after things for us."

"That's a relief." The tension humming through my body eased. Max ran his own pirate tour business through the late spring and summer months, which wouldn't open for a few more weeks. His salesmanship, not to mention his charismatic personality, ensured that the shop was in good hands and would most likely see an influx in sales. If he wore his pirate outfit, and odds were good that he did, the customers would be even more enchanted with him.

"Now, if you don't mind, we're going to check out the place," Grams said as she patted my cheek. "Come on." She hooked her arm through Roy's and Mattie's, then led them away from the group.

With that concern out of the way, I took a moment to peruse the gallery's interior and took note of the other attendees. The locals, especially those who owned businesses, were great about showing support to scheduled events and newcomers. I saw several shop owners whom I'd worked with on various committees throughout the past few years moving about the room, stopping to view the artwork hanging on the wall.

Kevin had done an excellent job with his remodel. The walls had all been painted white. Two-sided display panels, also done in white, were strategically situated at different angles in the center of the room. They were mounted on rollers and spaced apart with plenty of room for viewing. Each panel contained one or more paintings, depending on the size of the artwork.

As I continued to survey the room, I located everyone from Roger's class. All of them were standing in different locations, not gathered as a group. Even Edwina had made an appearance, though I thought it was a little odd since she was the only person I'd spoken with who hadn't mentioned anything about the gallery or the opening.

Ethan looked a lot different wearing a casual dress jacket and pants rather than the coveralls he'd had on at Hank's. A woman, close in age, stood next to him and intently listened to what he was saying about the painting they were viewing.

Polly was alone and standing on the opposite side of the room, periodically giving Amos and Sophie a wary glance. After her reaction the night before, I still couldn't tell if her nervousness was caused by the presence of one or both of them.

"There's Kevin," Jade said, glancing toward the opposite side of the room where he was talking to several of his guests. None of their faces were familiar, and I wondered if they were artists from other locations in Maine. According to Grams, Kevin's business had been quite successful before he'd relocated to Cumberpatch. It only made sense that some of his clients had followed him, or at least their artwork had.

Kevin must have sensed Jade looking at him because his amber eyes lit up the second he saw her. He excused himself from the people surrounding him and strolled over to join us. "I'm so glad you could make it." He smiled at Jade, and as an afterthought, pulled his gaze away and included the rest of us.

"Thanks for inviting us," I said, even though I had a feeling Jade's attendance was what he cared about the most. "The place looks great."

"Thank you. It turned out better than I expected," Kevin said. "If Evelyn was still here, I think she would have liked it as well." It had been some time since I'd talked to Kevin. If he missed his aunt, which I was certain he did, there was no hint of it in his cheerful voice.

"Detective," Kevin said, holding his hand out to Logan.

"I'm not on duty tonight," Logan said, returning the shake. "Please, call me Logan."

Kevin acquiesced with a nod. "As you can see, I have plenty of pieces on display." He swept his hand across the room. "You can't see it from here, but on the other side of those panels,"—he shifted to draw our attention—"is a section highlighting the Cumberpatch artists. And over in the corner are some tables with beverages and snacks if you're interested."

"The snacks wouldn't happen to be of the sweet variety, would they?" Shawna asked before I could.

"They came from Mattie's place, so I'm sure you'll find some of your favorites," Kevin said.

"Awesome," I said before I could stop myself.

Logan chuckled and placed a hand on the small of my back. He didn't have to say anything for me to know he was thinking about grabbing a sweet or two himself.

Shawna and Nate didn't need any additional encouragement to leave in search of the snack table. I was torn between following them or doing some much-needed reconnaissance. I'd be able to enjoy the event a lot more if I could locate Roger's missing painting first. If there was food, I was counting on the majority of people in attendance to stop by the tables Kevin had pointed out before moving on to peruse the artwork.

Showing up with a member of local law enforcement could make investigating more difficult. Logan might be off duty, but people would be guarded with their answers if he was standing with me when I asked questions.

I didn't have to worry about my family and friends, which extended to the spoofers. They'd spent enough time around Logan since we'd started dating that they'd gotten to know him, and his profession no longer intimidated them.

Logan and Kevin's chat was the perfect opportunity to slip away and check out the section for local artists. "If you'll excuse me, I'm going to go look around," I said.

"Sure," Logan said, giving me one of his non-boyfriend warning looks.

It wasn't like I was going on a clandestine operation or entering someone's home in a less than legal manner, both of which my friends and I had done in the past. I'd thought about rolling my eyes but chose to return his gaze with an innocent flutter of my eyelashes instead.

I would've urged Jade to go with me, but she seemed content to be hanging out with Kevin, and I didn't want to ruin it for her. Besides, if I found the painting we were searching for, it wasn't going to magically disappear before I could tell her about it.

Thinking about things vanishing drew my attention to Roger. I hadn't reminded him to behave himself and was glad to see him hovering not far from our group. I didn't want to draw any strange looks, so I signaled my intentions by subtly tipping my head, then pulled out my phone and placed it next to my ear as I walked past him.

"Where are we going?" Roger asked.

"I want to check out the display for local artists."

"Okay," he said, falling into step next to me.

All of the artwork I passed had labels displayed beneath them. Each one listed the artist's name and the title they'd given their work. The information also included the medium used, such as oil or acrylic. Below that was the price if the artwork was for sale.

"Let me know if you see the one we're looking for," I

said. With any luck, getting a visual would help with his hazy memory.

"I will," he said, then glided more than he walked to the opposite end of the display.

Roger's work was well-known in Cumberpatch and the surrounding towns. Kevin had found several more people besides the ones on my list to loan their paintings to the gallery. He'd used Roger's artwork as the focal point, then lined the walls on both sides with works from other local artists.

Instead of a price on the labels posted below Roger's painting, it had the words "On loan by owner" followed by a name. The two paintings I was most interested in were the ones owned by Ethan and Polly.

I didn't need to spend time reading labels to find them because the painting with a soft luminescent glow was obviously the one I wanted.

I muttered, "I don't believe it" before I could stop myself, then glanced around to make sure no one had heard me. I stepped closer to get a better look.

After discovering my skill to see ghosts came with additional magic, specifically the ability to see residual essence, I knew what was on the canvas.

"Rylee, what's wrong?" Roger asked, returning to my side. He followed the direction of my stare and grinned. "That's the one. I knew you'd find it."

The painting was a seaside view and looked a lot like the picture hanging in my living room, except with subtle differences. The main one being the glowing crimson hue that appeared on different areas as if someone had dabbed the surface. Whatever magic had been applied to the painting had faded, which probably meant it had been a while since its application. Determining how long would be difficult, but instinctively I knew it had to be around the same time Roger died.

And if I was right, I was looking at the first real connection I had to his death. I didn't know who put it there or what it meant, but I was determined to find out.

I'd recently learned that essence could be seen in various colors, and each shade meant something different. Blue was the first color I'd seen that had been transformed into a poison after someone had enchanted a sleeping potion.

I wasn't familiar with this shade of red, what it was used for, or if it had harmful properties. The painting had been handled a few times since Roger's death. I assumed if whatever had been applied to the surface had been dangerous, then it was either no longer toxic or had a different use altogether.

Lavinia, the owner of the Mystical Moon, an apothecary and potion shop in Waxford Bay, who I'd met via the Haverstons, was the only person I knew who could provide with an answer.

I thought about the meeting Jade, Shawna, and I had scheduled for tomorrow, provided we were successful in finding the missing painting this afternoon. Our plan included searching for Roger's hidden clues and piecing them together. After finding the painting and discovering the essence, I figured it would also be a good time to call Lavinia and see if she knew what we were dealing with.

In the meantime, and because I couldn't take the painting with me, snapping several pictures with my phone would have to suffice.

Kevin probably had stringent rules about photographing the paintings. I didn't want to get caught, especially by Logan, who I expected to come looking for me any second. I lowered my phone and pretended to read something on the screen as I pulled up the right app, then aimed the lens and pressed the button. I'd forgotten about the clicking noise the phone made every time it took a photo and groaned.

Hearing my name, followed by a tap on the shoulder, had me squeaking and holding down the button. By the time I removed my thumb, I was pretty sure I'd gotten some good pictures of the floor, maybe even the tops of my shoes. I wasn't about to check, not with Edith Haverston standing next to me.

"Rylee, is everything okay?" Edith's sister Joyce, who was standing next to her, asked, sounding just as concerned. Though they'd startled me, I was impressed that I hadn't jumped or tossed my phone in the air.

I'd expected to see them dressed in black since it seemed to be their signature color, at least most of the time. Tonight, however, they'd deviated from what I considered normal. Edith wore a cobalt blue dress that accented her eyes, while Joyce had gone with a similar style in a deep burgundy.

I'd wanted to respond with a not really, but stopped myself before saying it out loud. Instead, I responded with a fine as I slipped my phone back in my purse and turned to face them. "Why do you ask?"

"Because I'm sensing the presence of one of your friends," Edith said, directing her gaze toward the area where Roger was standing.

"Only the passing of this one wasn't recent," Joyce added.

Part of me wanted to ask them how they always seemed to know when a new ghost popped into my life. Another part of me decided it was a question better saved for another time.

"You can tell Joyce and Edith that it's me if you want," Roger said, moving closer and smiling at the sisters.

I was shocked to hear that Roger knew them. I'd never seen him hanging out with others and assumed he liked to keep to himself. Was there a paranormal enthusiast hidden somewhere inside him?

I glanced around to make sure no one was within hearing distance before whispering, "Roger said to tell you hi."

I'd expected a gasp, or at least to hear an oh my, not the frowns I received from both of them.

"So, his death wasn't natural after all," Edith said as if she'd already done some speculating about the accuracy of his passing.

"Not if Rylee can see him," Joyce said.

It felt good to know I was right about that particular ghostly rule.

Voices from others slowly moving in our direction drew my attention. The time I'd anticipated for people to visit the food table hadn't lasted long. Now that the sisters knew about Roger, I didn't want to end the conversation. There was a good chance they could provide me with valuable insight. Insight that I didn't want anyone else to overhear. "Would you mind coming with me?" I asked.

"Not at all," Edith said after sharing a conspiratorial smile with Joyce.

After finding a more secluded location near one of the movable panels, I spent the next few minutes giving them a brief version of everything I'd done and learned since Roger first appeared in my living room.

"Is there anything else you'd like to add?" I asked, glancing over my shoulder to where I'd last seen Roger, and noticed that he was gone.

My irritation must have shown on my face because Joyce asked, "Is there a problem?"

"I can't believe he disappeared again," I grumbled, hoping he'd left the building rather than gotten bored and decided to amuse himself by moving objects.

Maybe he'd gone to find Grams. When it came to tormenting someone with his pranks, my grandmother seemed to be his favorite person. I strained to listen and was glad when I didn't hear any out-of-the-ordinary commotions.

Thinking about Grams reminded me of the rumors she'd heard regarding Sophie. Edith and Joyce had magical connections in the community, maybe even some powers I had yet to discover, and might know something helpful.

Talking about the paranormal as if it had always been a

part of my everyday life still felt strange, but it didn't stop me from asking, "Do you know Sophie Newsam?"

"We do. Why?" Edith asked.

"I heard she practices witchcraft," I said. "Do you know if it's true?"

Joyce and Edith didn't seem to mind my straightforward approach. They shared a knowing smile, then Joyce answered first. "As far as we know, she dabbles."

"Was there a reason you wanted to know?" Edith asked.

"I'd heard Amos had been unfaithful and that she used magic to end the affair," I said, purposely leaving out that Grams had been my gossip source.

"I do remember hearing something about Amos and Polly," Edith said. "But I don't know if Sophie was upset enough to use magic to end the discretion."

If Polly was the other woman, it explained why she'd acted strangely when I'd asked her about the Newsams and why their presence agitated her.

I was about to ask the sisters if there was anything else they might know but was interrupted by Shawna calling my name. I turned to see Nate and her hurrying toward us. "The brownies you like were going fast, so I snagged you a few," she said, holding out a small paper plate with artist designs scrolled around the edges.

By a few, she'd meant four, which I greedily eyed before taking the plate. Each square of delectable goodness was frosted with dark icing and made my mouth water. "Have I mentioned lately what an awesome friend you are?" I asked.

"Probably not," Shawna stated in a matter-of-fact tone, then giggled. "Hey Joyce, Edith. Are you enjoying the opening?"

"We are," Joyce said.

"Did Rylee tell you about her, you know...new friend?" Nate asked the sisters.

"She did," Joyce said.

"And we were about to tell her we'd be glad to help," Edith said.

"Help with what?" Logan asked as he moved to stand next to me. "Ladies." He acknowledged Edith and Joyce, then smiled when he spied my plate. "I hope at least one of those is for me."

It was a good thing I really liked the guy and didn't mind sharing with him; otherwise, I would've smacked his hand when he snatched a square from my plate.

Whatever help the sisters planned to offer, along with what I'd seen on Roger's painting, was something that needed to be discussed in private, so I changed the subject. "Where's Jade?" I asked Logan, hoping to distract him from questioning Joyce and Edith further.

"Kevin offered to give her a personal tour," Logan said.

"Speaking of tours…" Joyce said.

"We should finish ours," Edith finished for her. "It was good seeing you all again."

I waited for the sisters to disappear around the panel. "I found the display for Cumberpatch artists."

"You did?" Shawna asked.

"Uh-huh." I draped my arm over her shoulder. I knew Nate and Logan wouldn't need any additional encouragement to follow us, so I started walking. "And there's a painting I *know* you'll want to see."

CHAPTER FIFTEEN

Like the beginning of most weeks, customers coming into the shop early on Monday mornings started off slow. Though a little reluctantly, Grams agreed to cover by herself so Jade, Shawna, and I could meet in my apartment and piece together the clues from Roger's painting. If Max had been available, she'd have called him to work in the store so she could spend time with us. If things got busy below, Jade and I were only a phone call away.

After printing out the best of the pictures Shawna and I had taken of both paintings, my friends and I gathered around my kitchen table. Jade and I were already dressed for work. Shawna was covering the lunch shift and had brought her uniform so she could head for work from here. Roger hadn't shown up yet, and I was getting concerned that it would take us a lot longer to find the clues without his help.

As far as I was concerned, the sleuthing part of my visit to the gallery the afternoon before hadn't been a total waste of time. I still had no idea who'd killed Roger but finding his painting had definitely been a win. After showing the artwork to Nate, Logan, and Shawna, my friend had discreetly stayed behind to take extra pictures as backups in case something had gone awry with mine.

There were things the handsome detective was better off not knowing, so while Shawna had done her covert thing with Nate, I'd walked around the gallery and discussed the artwork with Logan.

Unfortunately, when we ran into one of my suspects, they'd reacted pretty much the way I'd expected. None of them had ever met Logan. As soon as they learned he was related to Roy, and the newest member of the law enforcement team, things went from friendly and welcoming to reserved and polite.

I'd hoped to get Logan's insight, or at least gauge the reactions of my suspects, but neither the topic of Roger nor his treasure ever came up in any of our brief conversations.

I'd been right about the woman with Ethan. She turned out to be his fiancée Anna, who was happy to share the details of their recent engagement and upcoming wedding, which eventually led to Ethan relaxing his rigid stance.

Amos had been his charming self, glad to point out that one of his paintings was on display and available for sale. Seeing me with Logan seemed to soften Sophie's attitude. She'd been a lot more cordial to me than she'd been the day before. It left me wondering if the sudden change was due to his job or learning that he was my boyfriend.

Polly was the only one we'd spoken with who didn't show signs of being apprehensive. She already knew Logan from the few times he'd gone with Roy to the cafe for lunch and was happy to visit with us.

Out of everyone on my list, Edwina was the one I'd wanted to talk to the most but didn't get the chance. I'd noticed her leaving during the conversation Logan and I had with Polly. I wasn't sure why it bothered me that Edwina hadn't said anything about the gallery's grand opening. It didn't matter what kind of event was taking place in Cumberpatch. The locals couldn't resist chatting about them. Maybe it was because she was an artist, and I'd assumed a new place to display her work would've been something worth mentioning.

"Sooo," I said to Shawna as I reached for the pot in my coffee maker and refilled my cup. "I noticed that Nate didn't have a problem spending time with you last night."

To get a better visual of all the details, I'd blown up the images and printed them on numerous sheets of paper, then lined them up along the center of the table's surface. Shawna had a scissor and was cutting off the white edges so we could fit them together accurately.

"That's because I was worried for nothing," Shawna said.

"Are you saying his strange behavior wasn't because he was cheating on you?" Jade asked. There was a note of smugness in her voice, and I expected to hear an I told you so any minute.

"No, it's because he was shopping for the perfect gift for my birthday and wanted it to be a surprise. Look what he got me." Shawna held out her arm, then shook her wrist, showing off a new charm bracelet.

"But your birthday isn't for another month," Jade said.

"I know, but he couldn't wait," Shawna said with a smirk.

I leaned closer, then lifted one of the silver charms to get a better look. "Is that a zombie?"

"Yep, and look, there's even a gargoyle," Shawna said, twisting the bracelet to show us another figure.

The way Shawna beamed meant Nate had scored a considerable amount of points with his gift. With one friend's love life back on track, I was anxious to hear how things were progressing for the other. "How about you?" I asked Jade. "How was your date with Kevin?"

"It wasn't a date, but I did have a good time," Jade said, her blue eyes shimmering.

"Not stellar?" Shawna asked. "Because good seems a little too weak to describe the way your face was glowing by the time we left the gallery."

I hated to miss a teasing opportunity, but Shawna's statement reminded me of the critical clue I hadn't shared with them yet. "Speaking of glowing," I said, setting my cup on the table and away from the papers. "I saw some residual essence on Roger's painting."

"No way," Shawna exclaimed, stopping the scissors mid-cut.

"Did it look the same as before?" Jade asked. She leaned forward, propping her elbows on the table and clasping her cup with both hands.

"No, the color was a deep shade of red and looked like it was part of the paint and dabbed onto the canvas," I said. "Which is why I want to give Lavinia a call and see if she can help us." I walked to the coffee table and retrieved the phone out of my purse.

"That's a good idea," Shawna said, then returned to trimming the sheet in her hand. "If anyone would know what we're dealing with, she would."

I scrolled through my contact list until I found the number for the Mystical Moon Apothecary and Potion Shop. After several rings, a female voice I didn't recognize answered. She spouted the name of the shop, then said, "This is Aria. How can I help you?" I'd visited Lavinia's shop once, and she'd been the only person there at the time. Running a business took a lot of work. It made sense that she'd have an employee or two.

"Hi, Aria," I said. "Can I speak to Lavinia?"

"I'm afraid she's out," Aria said. "If you want to leave your name and number, I'll have her call you as soon as she gets back."

I had no guarantees that Lavinia would be able to help, but I was still disappointed that I'd have to wait for an answer. After giving Aria my information, I returned to my seat in the kitchen and set the phone on the table.

"Maybe it won't take her long to call back," Jade said, after noting my displeasure.

I fidgeted with the two sheets of paper Shawna had already trimmed. Both of them belonged to the painting I owned. I had finished laying them on the table and matching the edges when a melodic tune erupted from my cell. My phone was sitting closer to Jade and made her jump. "Told you." She released a nervous laugh to hide the fact that she'd jostled her cup and almost spilled her coffee.

I hurried to grab the phone, my momentary rush of excitement fading when I saw Bryce's name on the screen. Not that talking to him wasn't equally important. "Hey, Bryce," I said after swiping to answer the call.

"Morning, Rylee," he said. "I'm sorry I missed seeing you last night. Nate told me the gallery had a good turnout."

"Kevin did a great job putting the event together," I said, glancing at Jade. Hearing Kevin's name had her smiling.

"How's the investigation going? Did you uncover any clues to help Roger?"

"As a matter of fact, I did," I said, then proceeded to tell Bryce about the essence I found on the painting.

"Wow, what did Nate say when you told him?" he asked.

"There were too many people around, so I didn't get a chance to tell him before Logan and I left. But you can tell him if you want," I added, saving Bryce the trouble of asking my permission. Everyone in the ever-growing group of people who knew about my spirit-seeing ability was good about checking with me first before sharing details, even with each other.

"Thanks," Bryce said. The spoofers were close, and I'd bet that Nate would be his next call once we were finished. "Have you thought about giving Lavinia a call? Maybe she can help like last time."

"I already did, but she wasn't at the shop. I'm waiting for her to call back," I said. "What about the poltergeist thing?"

"I talked to my buddy James who lives in Portland. He said there are a few documented occurrences where magic was involved in the death, but there's no definitive proof available to prove one way or another."

"So we're back to speculating," I grumbled.

"Sounds like it," Bryce said, sounding more disillusioned than I was.

"Were you able to find out whether or not Roger is going to be trapped here permanently?" I asked, needing some good news, no matter how small.

"James wasn't absolutely sure on that one either. He said if magic is involved, the normal rules governing spirits could change, but he felt confident that the odds were favorable Roger would move on if the issues surrounding his death were resolved."

"It's not great, but I'll take it," I said, sounding as hopeful as I felt.

"I can keep researching if you think it will help," Bryce said.

"No, that's all right. You've done more than enough, and I'm grateful."

"Um, Rylee, before you go..." There was a long pause from Bryce's end of the line, and I visualized him running his hand along the side of his head.

"Yes?"

"I wanted you to know I did something you may or may not be happy about," Bryce said.

"What would that be?" I asked, unsure what he could've done to cause the anxiety I heard in his voice.

"Shawna told me about the website she found with the sleuther certification and asked me if I'd heard of it," Bryce said. "I hope you don't mind, but I also asked James if he knew anything about it."

"It's okay." Surprisingly, I didn't mind and was curious to hear what he'd learned. "What did you find out? Is it legitimate or a scam?" I'd been leery about it being the latter, which was part of the reason I hadn't pursued it any further.

"James swears the guy running the organization has quite a bit of experience dealing with the supernatural. He also said there's a lot involved in getting one of their certifications, and they're picky about who they let into the program." Bryce stopped, and I could hear him puffing out a breath. "Maybe you *should* check it out."

I hadn't spent much time perusing the site when Shawna had showed it to me and didn't realize they offered more than one kind of certification. "Maybe I will, and thanks for letting me know."

"No problem," Bryce said. "I'll talk to you later."

"What did Bryce have to say about Roger?" Jade asked after I'd disconnected the call.

"Nothing conclusive," I said, returning my phone to the table. "It's possible magic is behind his ability to move things."

"And helping him move on?" Shawna asked.

"Also a possibility."

"That's a good thing, right?" Jade asked.

"Yeah, but only if we can solve his murder," I said.

Telling my friends what Bryce had learned about the sleuther certification would lead to a lengthy discussion, so I decided to save it for later. Maybe after I'd done some research of my own first. Instead, I decided to catch them up on what I'd learned from Joyce and Edith. "I ran into the Haverstons last night and found out some interesting news."

"Which was?" Jade asked.

"Remember the odd way Sophie was acting when we went to visit Amos?"

"You mean when she insinuated that we were there to steal her husband?" Shawna asked.

"Yeah," I said. "It turns out that Amos and Polly might have been having an affair around the same time Roger died."

"I don't remember the sisters saying anything about that," Shawna said, sticking out her bottom lip.

"It was before you brought me those delicious brownies." I thought it was important to continually let my friends know how wonderful they were.

"That might explain why Polly had acted so strangely when you said something about Roger renting from the couple," Jade said, then sipped her coffee.

"I thought the same thing," I said. "I even asked Joyce and Edith if they'd heard the rumors Grams had mentioned."

"The one about Sophie using magic to end the relationship?" Shawna asked as she picked up the last sheet of paper and began trimming.

"Uh-huh, but they hadn't heard anything," I said. "Even if they did, I'm not sure how it ties into Roger's murder."

"Not a useful clue then," Jade huffed.

"I know you're waiting to talk to Lavinia," Shawna said. "But I was thinking. What if the essence you found on the painting was a poison and had something to do with Roger's heart attack?" She made a final snip, then set the scissors on the table.

"Let's say you're right," Jade said. "How do you think they're connected?"

"Roger did say someone had been messing with his stuff, and after talking to Ethan, you thought it was him," Shawna said to me.

"Correct," I said. "I'm guessing you have another theory."

"I do." Shawna grinned. "What if Ethan wasn't the only one who'd gone through Roger's things?" She snapped her fingers. "What if someone put something in one of the paint tubes before his finger painting class?"

"That sounds plausible," Jade said. "If a toxin was responsible for Roger's death, then it had to be ingested or absorbed through the skin to work."

"I wondered the same thing," I said. "I decided to do some online research before going to bed after Logan dropped me off last night. All the information I found stated that artists usually wear nitrile or latex gloves to protect their hands while painting."

"The information is correct," Roger said, appearing in the middle of my kitchen. He was getting much better at poofing into my apartment and missing all the furniture.

I announced his arrival with a good morning. He was back in artist mode and wearing another apron. This one was a bright turquoise covered with splotches of yellow and purple paint.

"I would've been here sooner, but I wanted to check on all our suspects," Roger said.

"When you say you checked on our suspects, does that mean I'm going to read about some unusual happenings related to these visits in the newspaper?" I asked.

He snorted at my playful mock. If he'd done something to frighten his former classmates, I doubted any of them would have reported the incident to the police or done an interview for the Swashbuckler Gazette. Least of all, the person responsible for Roger's death.

"Did you learn anything interesting?" Jade asked.

"Sadly, there aren't any new developments," Roger said, then pulled out an empty chair away from the table and settled into the seat.

I shook my head in answer to her question.

"We appreciate your recon efforts, and since you're here," I said, sweeping my hand over our pieced-together creation. "We could sure use your help extracting the clues." Roger's memory, specifically regarding the details surrounding his treasure, was slowly getting better. Maybe if he saw the paintings laid out next to each other, he'd remember the clues more clearly. If not, what little sleuthing skills my friends and I possessed were going to get a workout.

I moved out of the way as Roger got out of his seat to

get a closer look. He rubbed his chin, glancing between the copies I'd printed of each painting. The one Polly owned showed a stretch of beach my friends and I were quite familiar with. Besides the occasional day spent sunning and playing in the water during our youth, we'd attended a few campfire parties. It was obviously the place we needed to start our search.

After leaning forward, so his face was inches from the print, he squinted. "See this?" he asked, tapping the paper. "I'm pretty the treasure is buried here."

Once the pictures were placed side-by-side, they'd formed a large X similar to those I'd seen on fake pirate treasure maps. I had to admire how Roger had blended the separate halves of the letter into each painting and made them look as if they were part of a rock formation. A formation that continued in both directions and made finding the exact spot we'd need to dig impossible without more clues.

The longer I stared at the area he'd pointed at, the more details I noticed. Like the shadows on the side of a boulder. "Is that a skull?" I asked, directing everyone's attention to the solitary rock midway into one of the paintings.

"And those are footprints, aren't they?" Jade asked, pointing at the small dark shapes that looked like a trail leading from my spooky rock to the spot Roger designated as the burial site.

Roger grinned as he gripped the straps of his apron. "Yep."

I repeated his affirmative answer.

"Geez, Roger," Shawna said after walking around the table and squeezing in between Jade and me. "It's impressive the way you did that."

"I agree," Jade said, smiling in Roger's general direction. "The detail is awesome."

It occurred to me that the only way he could have gotten the clues to match up so well was to have the two canvases sitting next to each other while he painted and why he'd been so adamant about finding the other painting.

"Now that we know *where* the treasure is buried, are you going to tell us what's inside?" Shawna asked.

Roger chortled. "Telling you would take all the fun out of looking for it."

It was hard to chastise him after realizing that this would be the last time he'd get to participate in a hunt, and even though my friends and I were substitutes for his niece, I wasn't about to ruin his fun.

"Oh, before I forget," Shawna said. "I think I may have found Erin."

"Really?" I asked. "Where?"

"On social media." Shawna gave Jade and me a look that said the answer should have been obvious. I didn't have to ask to know she'd spent a considerable amount of time searching the Internet.

"And?" Jade asked, rapidly bending the fingers of her right hand. "What else did you find out?"

"I couldn't find an address, but from the information and pictures Erin posted on her page, it looks like her parents moved to Florida, and she stayed behind to attend the community college here in Cumberpatch." Shawna folded her arms across her chest. Her mischievous grin made me wary because it usually preceded trouble. Even more so when Jade joined her, and they both focused their attention on me. "What do you think about asking Logan if he can help us find her?"

How was I supposed to say no, or tell them I wasn't comfortable with the idea, with Roger staring at me with a hopeful look.

Logan took his detective duties seriously, and I wasn't sure if doing a favor for his girlfriend would cause a problem. "I guess I could ask him," I said, my voice filled with trepidation.

"I appreciate it, Rylee… Thank you," Roger said.

"Don't thank me yet. I can't guarantee Logan will agree to help." I reached for my phone, not to call Logan, but to snap a few pictures of our newly found clues, then asked, "How do you guys feel about going on a treasure hunt after work today?"

CHAPTER SIXTEEN

Jade, Shawna, and I always participated in the town's annual treasure hunt during the Founders Day celebration. They were usually more excited than me about the prospect of finding one of the small wooden chests filled with fake doubloons.

Today, however, was different. Time should have passed quickly since the shop had quite a few visitors, mostly tourists, but it didn't. By the time I locked the front door, my body was pulsing with excitement and laced with anxiety. I was eager to search for Roger's treasure but worried, even with the clues, that we wouldn't find it.

This was one adventure Grams refused to miss. After stopping by her place to retrieve a shovel from the shed in her back yard, I stuffed it in my trunk, then drove us to the beach Roger had portrayed in his painting.

My friends and I hadn't visited the place since the end of last summer when we'd sat around a fire roasting marshmallows while Bryce and Myra used night vision goggles to see if they could see a ghostly pirate ship. Our expedition had been the result of a reported sighting by a group of teenagers. It had been a fruitless effort for the spoofers, but we'd all had a good time, anyway.

"Any sign of Roger yet?" Grams asked as she got out of the car.

"Nope," I said after glancing around the paved parking lot and noting two other unoccupied cars but no ghost. I wasn't worried. So far, when Roger said he'd meet me somewhere, he'd shown up...eventually. "Maybe he's already down on the beach," I added since our destination couldn't be seen from where we were standing.

"Then let's get going," Grams said. "We only have a couple more hours of daylight left."

"Don't worry," Shawna said, patting the lime green backpack draped over her left shoulder. It was the same one she'd carried around all through high school and was now officially used on all our investigating adventures. "I brought along flashlights, just in case."

Flashlights or not, I didn't want to be searching or digging in the dark. After retrieving the shovel, I waited for everyone to set their purses inside the truck for security purposes, then tucked my phone in my jacket pocket, and trailed after my grandmother.

The air was cool and filled with the low rumble of water splashing against rocks from the white-capped waves rolling in from the ocean. If we weren't on a mission, I'd plant my backside in the sand and take a few seconds to breathe in the salty air, and let the scenery lull me into a relaxed state.

Unfortunately, my grandmother had other ideas and was determined to keep our group moving. "Come on," she said, tugging on my jacket sleeve, urging me to keep up with everyone else.

Shawna had taken the lead. She held her phone out in front of her and used the pictures I'd sent her and Jade of the clues we'd found on Roger's paintings. "I think the starting point is somewhere around here," she said.

"Do you think the footprints on the painting were literal?" Jade asked after stopping next to Shawna to study the screen on her phone.

"What do you mean?" I asked, peering over Shawna's other shoulder.

"Do we need to find the spot where they start, then count out each of them?" Jade waved her hand in the general direction of the nearby rocks. "You know, like the pirates do in the movies."

"Roger went to a lot of trouble to reenact a treasure hunt for Erin, so it wouldn't surprise me if we did," I said.

"If that's the case, then I think that's the place we need to begin," Jade said, pointing at a nearby boulder with grass growing along one side of it.

I moved closer and pushed some of the blades aside. Sure enough, the eyes and mouth of a scary skull had been painted in black on the rock's hard surface. Time had faded the artwork but hadn't erased it completely. During the late spring and summer months, numerous people walked along this stretch of beach. I contemplated how many, if any, of them had noticed the skull. "I'd say you're right about this being the place we start," I said.

"You have to give Roger points for ingenuity," Grams said.

"How many footprints are on the painting?" I asked.

Shawna tapped the screen, then enlarged the photo. Her lips moved, so I knew she was silently counting. "It looks like there are exactly twenty-five of them."

We needed to be as accurate as possible. "Jade, you're the closest in height to Roger. Why don't you count off the steps," I said.

"Okay," Jade said, moving to stand as close to the boulder as possible. When she began taking steps, Shawna, Grams, and I counted out loud and paced along with her.

By the time she'd taken her twenty-fifth step, we'd reached a place in the rock formation that stood at least five feet high and stretched out three times the same distance in either direction. In the sand near the rock's base was a hand-made letter X made out of flat stones in varying shades of brown and gray. It looked too fresh to have been created at the same time as the skull.

"This has to be the spot, right?" Shawna asked, a hint of uncertainty in her tone.

Grams bent down to get a better look. "There's no way that could've been here all this time, not without someone noticing it," she said as she straightened.

"Not to mention the destruction it would've sustained from the weather," Jade said. "I'd expect some of the rocks to be covered with sand or washed away."

"I agree," I said. Cumberpatch was located near the ocean. Our town received numerous rainstorms throughout the year, some of them less than pleasant.

"You don't think this is a prank, do you?" Shawna asked, then squinted at the screen on her phone again. "Because according to the clues on the painting, this looks like it's in the right place."

"I suspect a certain ghost is the culprit," I said, scanning the rest of the beach in search of Roger. A light gray pebble about the size of a quarter skipped across the sand and landed near my feet. "What the..." I said, backing up when two more seemed to dance in the air before following, one after the other, in the first stone's wake. I gripped the handle of the shovel, ready to use it as a bat if it looked like a stone might hit me.

"Roger," I scolded when his pale blue form appeared wearing his detective garb. "I thought you were going to show up earlier so you could help us."

It was a good thing I didn't overreact, and Roger couldn't sustain any damage; otherwise, I would've also pointed out how wrong it was to startle someone carrying a tool that could be used as a weapon.

"I would've if you'd needed me," Roger admitted smugly. "You all have been putting so much effort into finding my killer that I didn't think you'd mind spending a little time having fun." He grinned. "Admit it. You were enjoying yourselves."

"Maybe a little," I said, then repeated what he'd said to

the group and gaining smiles from everyone, myself included.

"I assume when you told me your treasure was buried, you actually meant it." I walked over to the spot he'd marked with the stones. For some reason, when I'd gone on previous hunts with my friends, I always ended up doing the digging. Since no one offered to take the shovel, I figured I'd been volunteered to be the designated digger again.

"There better not be a dead body buried here," I said after tossing aside my first shovel of sandy dirt and some of the stones forming the X.

He snickered. "Guess you'll have to keep digging to find out." Then, after softening his tone, he said, "It's not very deep, so please be careful."

"I will," I said, then spoke to Grams and my friends, directing most of my attention to Shawna since she shared an exuberant desire to see the undead. "Sorry, no dead body or zombies."

"Aww," Shawna groaned. "That's too bad."

"Unbelievable," Jade mumbled and rolled her eyes.

Grams snorted but didn't say anything, which made me wonder if she harbored a similar fetish she'd never mentioned.

After removing several more scoops of dirt, I heard a thump and felt the shovel's tip connect with something solid. Even though I'd been careful not to get overly ambitious with my efforts, I hoped I hadn't caused any damage.

"Here," I said, handing the shovel to Jade. The only way to get whatever Roger had buried out of the hole was to get down on my knees and push away the remaining dirt with my hands. It would've irritated me to ruin a good pair of work pants, and I was glad I'd changed into jeans before we left the shop.

It didn't take me long to uncover a thick layer of clear plastic coating the rounded lid and sides of an ornate wooden chest the size of a jewelry box. When Roger hid his treasure, I didn't think he expected it to be buried longer than a day or two. He'd still taken great care to ensure the contents had remained sealed against the elements.

Once I got the chest out of the hole, I placed it on the ground next to me. Everyone crowded around me expectantly, even Roger. "Is it still all right?" he asked, his playful expression replaced with concern.

I undid the tie used to keep the bag shut, then peeled back the plastic. "It appears to be okay," I said, then double-checked by running my fingers along the surface, feeling for nicks in the wood and searching for signs of water damage.

"That chest looks old," Jade said. She was leaning forward with her hands on her knees. "Is it an antique?"

"My father found it at an auction years ago," Roger said. "I inherited it when my parents passed away."

I relayed what he said, then asked, "Do you mind if I open it?" My friends and I had put a lot of work into finding the chest. The thought of finally seeing what was inside had my fingers tingling with anticipation.

"Please, go ahead." Roger already knew what I'd find but sounded as anxious as I felt.

After undoing the latch, I slowly lifted the lid, drawing out the moment and gaining irritated groans from the group. Before Grams issued a warning or decided to thump the back of my head, I pushed it open the rest of the way and gaped at the contents.

A velvety blue cloth lined the bottom of the box. On top of it sat four gold coins, similar to the ones I'd seen on display in the Cumberpatch Cove Pirate Museum. "Are those real doubloons?" I asked, astonished and curious as to how they'd ended up in Roger's possession.

"Yes," Roger said. "They're Spanish doubloons and in good condition. The last time I had them assessed, each one was approximately three-thousand dollars in value."

"Three-thousand each…seriously?" I gasped. I wasn't a collector, nor did I know how much the value of an object changed from one year to the next. Since it had been a few years, I assumed that each coin was worth a little more now.

He nodded. "They've been in my family a long time, which is why I was worried that someone might have stolen them."

"I'm curious," Grams said. "If they're worth so much money, why were you turning their care over to a sixteen-year-old?"

"Erin was mature for her age and quite responsible," Roger said a bit defensively. Clearly, he loved and adored his niece. "She had the same fascination with collecting things like my father and would've enjoyed them much more than I did. Since I never had any children of my own, I wanted her to have them and not wait until I was dead to enjoy them."

As I shared what he said with the group, I noticed pinks and yellows had appeared in the sky. It wouldn't be long before we lost sunlight. "We can keep this at my place until we locate Erin," I said as I closed the lid and secured the latch. I shook as much of the dirt off the plastic bag as I could, then resealed the chest inside.

Once I'd gotten to my feet and dusted off my pants, Shawna pulled a packet of wet wipes out of her backpack, then held one out to me. I was tempted to ask her what else she'd stashed in her bag since the last time it had been used but changed my mind. When it came to my friend, there were things I'd rather not know.

"Thanks," I said, wiping the grit from my skin, then tucking it in the pocket of my pants, intent on tossing it in a trash receptacle as soon as we reached the parking lot.

After picking up the chest, I noticed that Jade had already filled in the hole. "Shall we?" I asked, motioning with my head toward the other end of the beach.

"We shall," Shawna said, once again taking the lead.

We were halfway to my vehicle when a muffled melodic noise came from inside my jacket. I set the chest on the ground near my feet, so I wouldn't have to juggle it to answer the call.

I read the name on the screen and smiled. "It's Lavinia," I said before answering.

"Hey, Rylee, I received a message that you called," Lavinia said, her voice pleasant and cheerful. "Please don't tell me you found another body or something covered with essence again?"

Lavinia's question reminded me that she possessed the same intuitiveness as Joyce and Edith. "There isn't a body, but I definitely found some essence that I think is linked to another murder," I said. "I thought you might be able to help me again."

"Absolutely," Lavinia said. "Tell me what you saw and why you think a death is involved."

Everyone, including Roger, had gathered around me and intently listened to my side of the conversation. "Do you mind if I put you on speaker?" I asked, not wanting to spend extra time repeating her side of the conversation. "Shawna and Jade, who you already met, along with my grandmother and Roger, my new ghostly friend, are standing here with me."

"Not at all."

I spent the next few minutes telling her everything that had happened, from Roger's appearance to his speculations about being murdered, and finishing with an in-depth description of the essence I'd seen on Polly's painting.

The last time we'd met, I got the impression Lavinia knew a good deal about the witching community. I was tempted to ask her what she knew about poltergeists but decided against it. I'd been too busy trying to solve Roger's murder and find his treasure that I hadn't gotten the chance to discuss the topic with him yet. I wasn't sure how he'd react to the news and didn't want him to hear about it from listening to my conversation with Lavinia.

Lavinia took a few moments to process everything I'd told her, then said with the seriousness of an expert, "From what you've described, it sounds like we're talking about the combination of potions and magic again. Only this one had deadly properties to begin with and was most likely the cause of Roger's heart attack."

"I knew it," Roger said.

"Lavinia, does the poison have to be ingested, or can it be absorbed through the skin?" I asked.

"Either, as far as I know."

"See," Shawna exclaimed. "I told you someone put something in Roger's paint."

"But if he was wearing gloves, how could the poison get into his system?" Jade asked.

"The enchantment used on the potion would have rendered their protection useless," Lavinia said.

"Do you know what kind of poison was used?" I asked.

"There's only one that I know of," Lavinia said. "And it is derived from the Monkshood plant, which is more commonly referred to as wolfsbane."

Hearing Lavinia repeat Edwina's words had a tightness building in my chest and my stomach churning. I didn't want to believe she was the killer, nor did I want to openly discuss the possibility while standing in the middle of a public beach.

"I've seen pictures of that plant before," Shawna said. "When it blooms, the flowers are purple, right?"

I clamped my lips shut and let Lavinia answer her question. A few seconds later, a bell tinkled in the background of wherever she was calling from, which I assumed was her shop. "I'm afraid I need to go," Lavinia said. "If there's anything else I can help you with, please don't hesitate to contact me."

"Thanks, we will," I said, then disconnected the call.

"I know that look," Grams said, placing a hand on my

arm. "You figured something out, didn't you?"

"Maybe," I said, still hoping I was wrong about Edwina. "Can we talk about it in the car?" I bent down to pick up the chest.

"Sure," Grams said.

Jade and Shawna also voiced their agreement. When I didn't get a response from Roger, I stopped and shifted sideways, only to find that he was gone. "Darn," I mumbled. I thought for sure he'd stick around now that we'd found his treasure and discovered how he'd been murdered.

"Roger left again, didn't he?" Grams asked.

"Yeah, but I don't know why," I said, plodding across the sand, each step feeling heavier than the last.

CHAPTER SEVENTEEN

By the time Shawna, Jade, Grams, and I had returned to my vehicle, the two cars I'd seen earlier were gone. After telling everyone what Edwina said to me about the flowers in her painting, we'd spent another half hour sitting in the lot and speculating before heading home.

None of us wanted to believe Edwina deliberately ended Roger's life. We struggled with devising any kind of plan to move forward. Other than accusing her outright, there was nothing we could do to prove whether or not she was guilty. In the end, sharing my suspicions with Logan was the best we could come up with.

It was nearing eight in the evening, too early to go to bed. Not that I'd be able to sleep if I had. Tension seemed to be my friend at the moment, so I settled on the couch, my laptop balanced on my lap, my phone sitting on the cushion to the right. It hadn't taken long for Barley to grow tired of tossing around his catnip-filled toy mouse and curl up against my leg on the left. I stared at the screen, unable to concentrate because my mind kept replaying everything I'd learned over the past few days.

I'd already sent Logan a text asking him to call me, so there wasn't anything else I could do as far as he was concerned, but wait.

I stared at the chest sitting on the coffee table and scratched Barley's head. "It's great that we found Erin's present, but I'm still no closer to proving Edwina is the person who killed Roger or why. She had no motive, and when I talked to her, she didn't believe his treasure was real."

It would've been helpful if Roger had stuck around or even showed up now, so I could ask him what he thought.

"And if the killer wasn't Edwina, why would someone trouble themselves with poisoning Roger without getting the map or finding a way to obtain the clues first?" I continued to use my cat as a sounding board.

I rubbed my temples. Nothing made sense, and rambling was making my head hurt. I was trying too hard to solve Roger's murder and needed a distraction. I remembered what Bryce had said about the sleuthing certification, so while I waited for Logan to call me back, I decided to check out the website Shawna had shared with me.

Things in my world, particularly the ghostly part of it, were constantly changing. Having broader access to the paranormal world would be useful. There was so much I didn't know, and I couldn't keep relying on others, especially the spoofers, to find answers. I knew Bryce didn't mind and was always happy, sometimes eager, to help.

If I was going to be dealing with the supernatural regularly, I needed to be better informed. Even if I never used the spirit sleuther certification to start my own business as my friends suggested, having access to the information it provided could be beneficial.

I scanned the information on the main page, then stopped on the section labeled "Continuing Education" for those already certified. Curious, I clicked the link and read the list of classes available. The first two that caught my eye were *How to Wield Magic 101* and *Demon Slaying for*

Beginners. I knew magic was real but struggled to process the fact that demons might actually exist.

When I reached the class for *Dealing With Unruly Spirits,* I immediately thought of Martin. That class alone would be worth getting certified. I returned to the home page and clicked on the button before I could change my mind.

A box appeared with a message.

Thank you for your interest in obtaining a spirit sleuther certification. To determine whether or not you qualify, you will be required to complete an extensive questionnaire/application.

The fact that applicants were vetted sounded promising. Unless all the questions on the application wanted to know my personal information like finances and such, there was a good chance Bryce's friend James had been right about the organization not being a scam.

I kept reading.

Please note that applications can take between four to six weeks to process. If you are still interested, click below.

"Okay, Barley, what do you think?" I asked, scratching his head behind his ears. "Should I get a certification or continue winging it?"

His response was a murpy meow which turned into a loud rumbling purr. "I'm taking that as a yes." I paused with my hand hovering over the enter key. A few more seconds and a deep breath later, I pressed the button and clicked confirm.

I'd expected to see an online form. Instead, it asked for my address, stating that the required documents would be sent to me. Most organizations did all their business correspondence online, so I was surprised to read that I'd receive an application by mail. It also meant having to wait, which was a little disappointing.

I filled in the required information and received a

notice containing a confirmation and a note thanking me again for my interest. I had barely finished shutting off the computer and setting it on the coffee table when my phone played a chime alerting me to a new text.

The message was from Jade, and it read, "Check this out. I found it on the gallery's website. Pay close attention to the garden near the bottom on the right."

I tapped on the attachment, and the screen filled with a painting of someone's backyard with a beach view. I enlarged the area Jade mentioned and saw an elaborately detailed portion of a garden. I didn't need to ponder the identity of the talented artist long because I found Amos's name scrawled in italics through a portion of the plants. Plants, that if I wasn't mistaken, looked a lot like wolfsbane.

My pulse raced as I gave the rest of the painting a closer look and realized it was a rendering of the beach behind Amos's home, only from a different angle. With Sophie's connection to the witching community, I'd bet anything that the garden was her creation.

Another text from Jade arrived, telling me that she and Shawna were on their way over. Before I could respond to her latest message, the tune I'd assigned Logan echoed through the room, and his name appeared on the screen.

"Hey," I said, answering his call.

"Hey, back," Logan said. "Is everything all right? You sounded a little stressed in your message."

I could hear traffic in the background and knew he was driving his truck, which had a hands-free phone system installed in the dash.

"Not really," I said, then told him about my conversation with Lavinia and everything I now knew about Edwina, Amos, and their connection to the wolfsbane.

A knock on the door had me getting to my feet. "Hold on, there's someone at the door," I said to Logan, then placed the phone on the coffee table before walking across the room. I didn't have a peephole and couldn't see who was outside, but after getting Jade's message, I assumed it had to be my friends, that they'd already been on their way here when I received the text.

Roger appeared next to me just as I reached for the handle. The "Don't" he issued, too late to stop me from opening the door.

Amos was standing there wringing his hands. His hair was mussed, and the skin beneath his eyes was dark as if he suffered from sleep deprivation.

"Amos, what are you doing here?" I asked after my initial shock faded.

"I know it's late," he said. "But I was hoping you had time to talk." He took a step forward, putting him inches from the door frame, then added, "It's important."

The insistence in his voice made me wary, and I'd thought about telling him to go away.

"Rylee, I don't think it would be a good idea to upset him," Roger said. "Maybe you should let him in."

Roger made a good point. Amos was bigger than me. If he was the killer, which appeared to be a strong possibility, I didn't think closing the door would stop him from forcing his way inside. Knowing Logan was still on the phone and my friends were on their way gave me the confidence to say okay and take a step back so Amos could enter.

"What did you want to talk to me about?" I asked after closing the door, then moving to keep him in the kitchen area and block his view of my phone.

"You know, don't you?" he asked.

"Know what?" I asked, failing to sound as ignorant as I'd hoped.

"The truth about Roger's death, that he didn't have a heart attack."

"He didn't?" I asked, sneaking a glance at Roger. He was leaning against the counter near the kitchen sink, his arms crossed, his expression contorted in anger.

"I heard rumors about you being a witch, but I didn't think any of them were true, not until you started asking questions about Roger, then showed up at the gallery opening with your cop boyfriend. When I saw you take pictures of his painting, I knew it was only a matter of time before you used magic to figure out that his death wasn't natural."

Apparently, my ability to appear inconspicuous needed work. There was no way for Amos to know I could see residual essence. He must have thought I could cast spells when he referenced using magic.

"Are your friends witches too?" Amos asked. "Were they helping you? Was that why you brought them to my place?"

"No, they don't have any powers, and they don't know anything," I said, embellishing the truth to protect my friends.

"So, how did you know?" Amos asked again.

"I had some spiritual help." Pretending seemed moot. When and if I got certified, everyone in Cumberpatch would know I could see ghosts anyway.

Roger grinned. "You're doing great. Keep him talking."

Encouraged, I asked, "Why don't you tell me what really happened to Roger?"

Amos's gaze glazed over. "You have to understand. Sophie's a good person." He rubbed the back of his neck and started pacing. "None of this is her fault. If I hadn't transgressed with Polly..." He stopped moving and gave me a pleading look. "It was an accident. Roger wouldn't have died if Polly hadn't loaned him her paint."

"I'd forgotten all about that," Roger said, pushing away from the counter.

"Paint?" I asked, remembering Shawna's theory.

"I was teaching a finger painting class, and Sophie knew if she put some of her special concoction in one of Polly's tubes that the gloves we were using wouldn't protect her."

From what I'd heard so far, Roger's treasure had nothing to do with his death. "To clarify, this whole thing was about you cheating, and Polly was the intended victim," I said.

"Yes, but I don't believe Sophie meant to kill Polly, only make her sick," Amos said.

"Sure she did," Roger grumbled.

I didn't think pointing out that Roger had ended up dead from his wife's attempt would change Amos's mind about what had happened. "If that's the case, then I'm sure Roy and Logan will be lenient on her," I said, realizing too late that mentioning local law enforcement was a mistake.

"No one is ever going to find out what Sophie…what either of us did," Amos growled through gritted teeth as he pulled a vial containing a purple liquid out of his coat pocket. "Because you won't be around to tell anybody."

I'd been so focused on backing up and putting some distance between Amos and me that I hadn't seen Roger open a cupboard door and pull out several coffee mugs. Not until the first one flew through the air and hit Amos in the shoulder.

"What the…" Amos's glare transformed into shock.

The next thing I knew, Logan had burst into the room with Shawna and Jade following close behind him. They had arrived in time to see Amos dodge another cup. It was a good thing Roger had grabbed cups from my plastic collection. If they'd done more than bounced when they landed on the floor, I'd be cleaning up a mess of broken porcelain and having to buy a new set.

"What's going on in here?" Logan asked after giving me an assessing glance to make sure I was okay.

Shawna and Jade stayed behind Logan but had moved to get a better view of Amos.

"Tell your girlfriend to stop," Amos said, waving his arms protectively in front of his body.

I raised my arm and swirled my hand as if I was the one

controlling the flying cups. Roger winked and shook the cup he was holding, which to everyone besides me, appeared as if it was magically floating through the air. Of course, Logan, Shawna, and Jade all knew it was Roger and did their best not to show any signs of amusement.

I didn't know how much Logan had overheard via my phone and wanted to make sure he got a full confession from Amos. "I will as soon as you give Logan the vial and tell him everything you told me about Roger's death."

CHAPTER EIGHTEEN

One Week Later

A lot had happened since the night Amos tried to kill me. After breaking down into regretful sobs and confessing what he'd done to Logan, Amos and Sophie had been charged with Roger's murder.

I'd later learned that Edwina's painting of the wolfsbane blossoms was created from pictures she'd taken during a visit to the Newsam's home.

Rumors and speculations ran rampant around town because Logan told Troy at the Swashbuckler Gazette that an investigation was started based on an anonymous tip. Logan had omitted mentioning my friends, me, and a paranormal connection during his interview for the article printed in the newspaper.

"Are you ready?" Logan asked, drawing me from my musing. We were sitting in his truck across the street from the house Erin rented with two other girls. After I'd told him she was still living in town, he'd used the system at work to find her address and phone number. He'd even offered to come with me once I scheduled a meeting with her.

"I think so," I said, patting the chest sitting on my lap.

"Take all the time you need," Logan said. He knew this was something I needed to do on my own and had offered to wait for me.

Maybe not entirely alone. The truck had an extended cab, and Roger was sitting in the back seat staring at Erin's house. He was dressed in the same outfit he'd been wearing when he'd first popped into my life. "Tell Logan thank you." It was the only thing he'd said during the entire trip.

"Roger wants you to know that he really appreciates you finding Erin for him," I told Logan.

Logan shifted in his seat to face Roger. "It's the least I could do after you saved Rylee's life."

Roger hid his embarrassment with a scowl. "Can we go before things get mushy?"

"Sure," I said, sliding out of the truck and heading for the sidewalk that would take us to the front door.

I'd seen several online pictures of Erin, courtesy of Shawna, and recognized her as the young woman who opened the door to greet us. "Rylee, right?"

"Yes," I said.

"Please, come inside." Erin led me into a living room, then motioned for me to sit on the sofa. The place was sparsely furnished and exactly how I'd pictured the home of three women working and going to college. If her roommates were home, I was glad they'd made themselves scarce for our visit. It was going to be hard enough answering Erin's questions.

"You mentioned finding something that belonged to my Uncle Roger," Erin said after taking a seat across from me.

"Roger gave my family a painting," I said. "I recently happened across a map hidden inside, so my friends and I decided to see if there really was a buried treasure." I handed her the chest. "We found this and thought someone in his family should have it. You were the nearest relative we could find."

Erin placed the chest on her lap and slowly lifted the lid with trembling fingers. "He told me he had a big surprise planned for my birthday, but this... It's not what I expected." She ran her fingertip across one of the coins, then swiped at the tear trickling down her cheek. "Thank you."

"You're welcome," I said, getting to my feet. Since there wasn't much more I could say, and I wasn't good with emotional moments, I didn't feel comfortable sticking around. "My boyfriend's waiting for me, so I should get going."

Roger had been standing off to the side. Now that his murder was solved and the last of his unfinished business was completed, it wouldn't be long before he moved on to the afterlife. He might not be able to talk to Erin, but I figured he might want to spend a little more time with her.

"Of course," she said, standing to join me. "I'll walk you out."

I'd made it across the street and had my hand on the truck's door handle when I heard Roger call my name.

I knew what was coming next and wasn't looking forward to it. "Yes," I said, proud that my constricted throat didn't cause my voice to crack.

"As much as I've enjoyed your sleuthing adventure, I'm ready to move on," Roger said. "Erin has her own life now and doesn't need an uncle who's a ghost hanging around, and I'm certain you don't either." He grinned. "Though it might be fun to pop down to Florida and see my sister and her husband. Maybe get in a little haunting action."

"Roger," I warned.

"I'm kidding." His tone sobered. "Thank you for everything you did. Please tell your friends and Abigail that I'm grateful for their help as well."

"I will." As Roger started to fade, I called after him, "Try to behave yourself, okay."

"I'm not making any promises." His laughter was the

last thing I heard before he disappeared completely.

ABOUT THE AUTHOR

Nola Robertson grew up in the Midwest and eventually migrated to a rural town in New Mexico where she lives with her husband and three cats, all with unique personalities and a lot of attitude.

Though she started her author career writing paranormal and sci-fi romance, it didn't take long before her love of solving mysteries had her writing cozies. When she's not busy plotting her next adventure, she spends her time reading and doing yard work.

Made in the USA
Coppell, TX
30 November 2021

66784189R00085